Nanonovels

Five-Minute Flash Fiction

Jules Horne

TEXTHOUSE
Scotland

Texthouse, Riverside Mills, Dunsdalehaugh, Selkirk, TD7 5EF
www.juleshorne.com

Jules Horne is hereby identified as the author of this work in accordance with Section 77 of the Copyright, Designs and Patents Act 1988.

Publisher's Note: This is a work of fiction. Names, characters, places, and incidents are a product of the author's imagination. Locales and public names are sometimes used for atmospheric purposes. Any resemblance to actual people, living or dead, or to businesses, companies, events, institutions, or locales is completely coincidental.

Cover Design: Victor Marcos
Book Layout ©2015 Joel Friedlander

Nanonovels/ Jules Horne. -- 1st ed.
ISBN 978-0-9934354-1-6

For Michael

Contents

Nanonovels

Nanonovels

Preface

NANONOVELS ARE SHORT stories written in five minutes, based on random stimuli taken from books and Google searches.

I wrote one a day from my birthday on 16th October, and the aim was to continue for a year, and see what I could learn about patterns, creativity and resistance.

The collection coincidentally captures a time in the early 21st century when we are being powerfully shaped by search engines. It also reflects an early 21st century bookshelf, and a human mind with all its faults, ruts and impulses, paddling through the English language towards a story.

INSTRUCTIONS AS FOLLOWS:
- Shut eyes.
- Go to bookshelf.
- Blind-choose book.
- Blind-open book and place your finger on the page.
- Open your eyes.
- Insert the word or phrase you find into Google. *This is the title of your story.*
- Open the first non-sponsored page that appears. Something on this page is your stimulus.
- Set a timer and write for five minutes.
- Stop.

You must always go with what turns up. Even - especially - if you spot another, more interesting, phrase on the page.

TWEAKS ALLOWED:
You may finish your sentence. You may tidy your spelling and correct grammar. If you aren't at home, you can go to a library and write your story there, using the same rules.

TWEAKS NOT ALLOWED:
You may not choose a different book, phrase, web page. Stick with what appears.

UNUSUAL SITUATIONS:
If the book page is blank, use another page.
If the web page doesn't display, use the 'page cannot be displayed' page.

FINDINGS:
You will always smile at the book you find. The web page, on the other hand, will always make you groan.
You will rediscover forgotten books.
You will discover books you have bought but never read.
You will discover books that someone else has bought, and you have never noticed.
You will discover books you have borrowed and forgotten to return.
You will leave rediscovered books lying prominently around the house.
Your bookshelf will become even more disordered.
Evening stories will write themselves differently from morning stories.

Introduction

Have you ever suffered from writer's block? If so, you may not know that there's a condition far worse: writer's *lock.*

This is a severe form of writer's block, characterised by *not doing any writing.*

When I began to write these nanonovels, I was suffering from writer's lock.

The condition had persisted on and off for a few months.

I wanted to write novels, plays, stories. But the enormity of the work ahead froze me into inaction. I'd wait until I had more time, I decided. Till things were quieter.

Of course, this never happened. The months and years were passing by. Writer's lock had a firm grip on my life. There came the point when I realised I wasn't even a writer any more.

Because writers *write*.

So on my birthday, 16th October, I decided to take things in hand.

Five minutes. That's all I'd do. So ridiculously easy that there could be no excuse.

But what if inspiration didn't strike? I devised a plan:

Stand before bookshelf. Shut eyes. Pick book. Open book and insert finger.

Read the words where your finger lands. This is the title of your story.

Insert these words into Google. Search. Go to the first non-sponsored page.

Something on this page is your stimulus.

Write for five minutes. Then stop. No editing.

For 150 days, I wrote a story a day in five minutes. These are the stories.

Below each story, you'll also find the book and web sources that inspired it.

It's best if you don't read too many nanonovels at once. They need time around them, like poems.

At the end, you'll find the story of how it ended. Along with some thoughts about nanonovels, randomness, writer's block and the creative process in general.

I hope you'll try the experiment and write some nano-novels of your own. You may not have a novel inside you. But you certainly have a nanonovel.

Free will is the sensation of making a choice.

—Brian Greene

Two Males

16 October

O UR DOGS ARE family raised and kid tested. The kids are specially chosen and trained. We look for kids with good poking fingers and curiosity. We look for kids that enjoy dragging their hands down the rough sides of walls. We look for kids that jump and scream and get themselves into a state of excitement. Then we bring on the dogs.

We choose dogs with the quietest temperaments, each parent as shy and accommodating as possible. Any trace of reactiveness, that pup is swiftly removed. The thicker that genetically passed on skin, the better. And then we toughen it up. We ask the jumpiest kids to jump, and those with the pokiest fingers to poke as jabbily as they can towards the dog's ears and eyes, building up cautiously to teeth. When the dogs can face being poked with small fingers in the teeth while their owner jumps and rubs them wrongwise from tail to brow, then we know they're ready to be sold.

We have two males ready to go. They look fairly steady from here.

James Patterson (2001). Violets Are Blue, p.233.
http://www.hoobly. com/0/0/469539.html.
Written in Jedburgh Public Library.

Jules Horne

Nourish

1 7 October

YOU MAY HAVE been trying for a while. You may have been on the brink of giving up many times. You may now be nearing 50, and see trying as an extreme reach of optimism.

The point when extreme optimism becomes delusion is unclear. Look in the mirror. See the wrinkles. That should give you a jolt. What baby wants to look up at her mother's face and see her grandmother's? That's why we've made this cream. It addresses the point where optimism becomes delusion, and shortcuts you straight into disillusion, followed (importantly) by grieving. It's important to mourn your unborn children, as well as the ones you almost had. The fictional children have as great a power to sadden as the ones who nearly made it. They're all milling around, jostling in your head, causing that extreme optimism.

It's a dangerous condition. It stops you getting on with life. You have yours still to live, even if your children don't.

Elizabeth Bishop (1983). Complete Poems, p.149.
http://www.nourish-fertility.com/

Merv Was Always

18 October

DESPITE HIS WEALTH, Merv was always a regular guy. He ate crispy crunches for breakfast, same as everyone else. The fact he sprinkled them with toasted diamonds was neither here nor there. He drove a tiny, second-hand Lear jet and had a poky mansion in the middle of Beverley Hills, where the neighbours were far too noisy in the night, and the garbage collectors rough and slapdash.

He toughed it out, and kept himself going, same as everyone else, with nights out in the caviar pub and occasional walks along the sides of gated neighbourhoods. He got old, same as everyone else, and bent over slightly, and found his voice more quivery than he felt.

He got to 82 and loved it there, and then died, same as everyone else. And now he lies in the ground, same as everyone else, just with a bigger, diamond-sprinkled headstone that draws jackdaws from far across the county.

David Mitchell (2006). *Black Swan Green*, p.173.
http://www.thecolumnists.com/jillian/jillianmurcia5.html

Jill Walking

19 October

T HEY HAVE A tiny pleat in front, and that's the problem. It bumfles.

- What do you mean, bumfles?

- It sticks out. I can cover it up with a jumper, but then the jumper bumfles.

- We can't take items back just because they bumfle. That word doesn't even exist.

- It does. We're both using it.

- It's not on the list of reasons for returning items. Soiling – that's a reason. Or tearing. Or bad finishing, such as loose thread hanging from the cuff which might get pulled and lead to the item unravelling.

- But why design a pair of shorts with a bumfle in the first place?

- It's a noun now, is it? A bumfle?

- Yes. And in fact, there are two. Plural.

- I can see about getting 'bumfling' added to the list if you like.

- That would be grand.

- But until then, I can't take the shorts back.

- How about if I pull on this thread here?

- That might be the short-term answer, Jill.

Alasdair Gray (1985). The Fall of Kelvin Walker, p.61.
*http://cgi.ebay.com/Fine-Linen-J-Jill-Walking-Shorts-sz-26W_*
WoQQitemZ150172456109QQcmdZViewItem

You Been Tellin

20 *October*

Tonight the streets are ours. They been cordoned off, special for us. I'm glad you put the gladrags on. The yella slip of a dressthing. And me in jaiket and tie all a-throttling.

Everyone inside. Everyone fearful in their TV rooms. Everyone feelin the hairs rise backo their necks as we pass them by. You stalkin. Me hoofin wi a kindo skip which I try to hide, for it wouldna be seemly.

We is lucky people. The streets are ours. Just tonight. And then tomorrow, they pass on to others. But tonight, we're safe. We can do anything, be anywhere, be anyone.

I am looking at that wall by the Golden Lion and seein it for the first time, wi no one else's shadow ont.

Only ours.

That wall is ours. Tonight and no time else.

Wanna make love? Wanna lean and watch the shadows pass?

Wanna dance? There's space enough. There's darkness enough.

You been tellin me long enough you wanna dance sometime.

*Annie Proulx (1996). Accordion Crimes, p.335. http://www.
lyricsmania.com/lyrics/niche_lyrics_9432/other_lyrics_30321/
youve_been_cheatin_and_tellin_me_lies_lyrics_329156.html*

Jules Horne

Thursday 0630

21 October

THE EMERGENCY DOCUMENTARY meeting started at 6.30. We opened with a midshot on the door as the participants arrived: directors, producers, researchers, camera teams. There were close ups on the flasks of coffee and the plates of tired biscuits, zooming in to a small round jammy dodger with the bay windows reflected in its shiny red jam.

However, no one was interested in biscuits. We panned around the table of grim, fixed faces as the meeting began – a handheld shot, taking in Kurt, Sewald, Johnston and Kerr – everyone who'd been part of the teams that made the world's most successful documentaries.

We landed on Martin, homed in on his eyebrows, his dark, hidden eyes, as he launched into the reason we were here.

There were no more stories, no more subjects. There was nothing left to film, except ourselves.

Dan Richardson (1989). Hungary, The Rough Guide, p. 101. http:// www.screeneditors.com/forums/showthread.php?threadid=1674

Twist

22 *October*

"**I**'M SORRY, BEN. You have a bad case of sylosis."

"What's sylosis?"

"It's a rare disease where your inside feels like your outside. The organs and tissue that are normally hidden from view feel raw and exposed, as though they are fully open to the outside, and all the air and dust that that entails."

"How did I catch it?"

"By being too attentive to it."

"So if I ignore it, it'll go away?"

"That's the gist of it."

"How can I ignore six feet of red raw groaning tissue? It bleeds constantly. It feels cold all the time, from the breezes. If I don't sit indoors away from draughts I shiver so bad my bones ache."

"Ignore it. And don't share it with your nearest and dearest. It's an off-putting sort of thought. They may avoid your company."

"But what about this heart? It flops around. It's painful."

"Put it in your breast pocket and take a couple of Aspirin."

WB Yeats (1991). Selected Poetry, p.145.
http://www.thetwist.co.uk/

Jules Horne

Overemphasize

23 *October*

Y OUR VOTES ARE noted and appreciated. They're unfolded, flattened and placed in piles. They're stacked side by side in an orderly fashion, rising pink blocks that show how very much you cared about turning up in your rows in the morning.

The queues went around the block, I'm told. They started to fold back on themselves and chaos threatened. We sent out men to unfurl the blockage, untooth the cogged crowds and send each wave off in its own direction. Throughout the morning and into the afternoon, they trudged forwards, inching, millimetering towards the entrance to the hall, where they were ticked off on the endless concertinaed form. Then off into the booths, where they shyly cradle their papers behind their arms, in the manner of schoolchildren during exams.

While your votes are appreciated, they are not counted. That's not the point of the exercise. We already know the result. The point is that you take part. Participation in the democratic process is all. I can't overemphasize this. It's what this nation is built on.

Paul Chanin (1993). *Otters, p.57.*
http://www.thefreedictionary.com/overemphasize

Under The Skirt

24 October

A M I A sexy secretary? I don't think I'm really the judge of that. I can show you the way excel spreadsheets slowly open, with rows and rows of numbers hinting at the promise of strange other worlds.

324230239
432432489
533920432.

I can slide my mouse along the tabs at the bottom and finger them with pixels, suggestively if you like, where other pages with new riches are hidden:

43290432
4329085
5402342.

And we could look together at charts – long, stretching bar charts, round, exploding pie charts, exponential curves and trend lines reaching off to places of the wildest imagination.

But above all, I could invite you into the furthest reaches of my mind, where neurons fire like small explosions, brainy things happen and I create the pictures that only will let you under my skirt.

Alan Warner (2002). *The Man Who Walks*, p.117.
http://community.webshots.com/album/282970248eIXhau

Jules Horne

Very Still

25 October

VERY STILL, NOW. Relax. Feel your arms grow heavier and heavier, their weight sinking into the ground. Loosen your back and let it sink, sink, the muscles releasing their hold. Let yourself fall deeper where you lie, the ground an earthen pillow, taking the mounting weight of your body.

Your jaw is too tense. Let it fall, let it fall. Let all the tension drift away. Your jaw is a heavy tool of bone, flopped into your drifted tissue. Let gravity take you deep down, your body soft and melding with the giving earth.

That twitch on your right eye – stop it. Curl up your eye and release it, curl and release. Let that twitch float free, up and up and into the sky. Do not watch it go. Shut your eye and feel the lids sink heavy and heavier on your eyeballs, pressing them deeper into your skull.

When you are heavier than you have ever been, just stop. Lie there.

There are no further instructions.

Liz Lochhead (1989). Mary Queen of Scots Got Her Head Chopped Off, p.67. http://www.pbs.org/wgbh/pages/frontline/ kevorkian/aboutk/art/still.html

Naturally Walden

WALDEN PRESS RELEASES:
New Oat Sack Arrives

Eagle Lands

Weather Turns for Worse

Trouser Knees Wear Out: Patches on Standby

Hole in Roof Drama Over

New Lichen Species Spotted

Bean Price Hike Due

Beans Drop Half-Cent

Conversation Stoppers: An Expert Guide

How to Cope With Flatulence

Tree Grows Another Ring

Roof Leak Mended: Second Time Lucky

Rain Stops Play

Beans Stop Play

Life Stops Play

Thoreau Plays: Shock Exclusive!

Albert Zuckerman (1994). Writing the Blockbuster Novel, p.83.
http://www.wiig.com/main/news70.htm

Jules Horne

Air With Smoke

27 *October*

Y OU CAN BECOME a child's hero. It's easy. You don't
even need to wear a special costume. Just lean over, in a
tall kind of way, and tell them how the world is.

They will believe you. It's very touching. You can tell them
the world is flat or cube or filled with garden fairies, it's all the
same to them. You can tell them it's round and spinning and
suspended in an infinite chasm of matter called space, and
they'll believe that too. It's all the same to them.

Imagine the responsibility! You can tell any stories you
want, and they'll be accepted. And yet you're the most unreliable storyteller in the world, for what the hell do you know?
How much have you experienced? How much have you actually seen, felt, lived through in the tight little jacket of the
world you schlep around with you?

Horrifyingly little. And yet you pass the stories on.

How irresponsible! How criminal! What damage you're
probably causing!

Best to avoid children entirely, or else be brutally honest
about everything you don't know.

Don't expect them to thank you.

Denton Welch (1950). *A Voice Through a Cloud*, p.105.
http://www.epa.gov/smokefree/

Access To Kilmory

28 October

EIGHTEEN RESIDENTS OBJECTED to opening access to Kilmory. Eighteen was practically everyone, from Mr Wight the fencer at the far end, to Mrs Devises, who lived on her own and was the nearest to the track.

The problem was the Christians. It wasn't that the residents were against religion or the religious – many of them went to church at Christmas and Easter and filled up heavy envelopes for the missing weeks in between, just in case there was anything in the theory of sin accounting.

It was the fact that the Christians were so in your face. They wore long hooded cloaks and carried crosses across their shoulders as they made the pilgrimage to Kilmory Rig. Usually the crosses were of light balsa, but some crazies went far beyond, with oak logs and the self-whipping. It was enough to put you off your breakfast. And there were hundreds of them – sometimes thousands, on weekends and holy days.

Mrs Devises was prepared to lie down in the track to stop it. The occasional fence hopper was bad enough, but the ceaseless streams were getting her down.

Magnus Magnusson (1988). Rum, p.47. http://www.north-ayrshire. gov.uk/ChiefExec/minutes.nsf/80fe3b34a1c42ddb8025708400347 ce4/a2a77fcb178cc1cb8025698a004eefe6?OpenDocument

Taylor's Theorem

29 October

Of course, it isn't Taylor's Theorem at all. It's Gregory's Theorem. As Taylor well knows.

We've had it out. Soon as he came up here, through the gates, past clearing, admin over and done with, I was onto him.

- You Brook Taylor?

- Surely, sir.

- The mathematician, Brook Taylor?

- Tis I.

- Well, I'm James Gregory. Yes, well may you blanche, sir. At least you have to good grace to do so. You know what it's about, of course?

- Can't say I do, sir.

- A little matter of a theorem.

- You are also a dabbler in the art of mathematics, sir?

- Dabbler? You have some nerve. That theorem of yours –

- Which theorem, pray?

- You know the one, damn it, sir. They call it Taylor's.

- Ah.

- Well, it isn't. It's mine. It's Gregory's. Forty years ago I came up with it, and did I get the slightest credit?

- I fear not, judging by your apoplectic expression.

- Sit down, sir. Pull yourself up a cloud. We shall both be here some considerable time.

Geoffrey Matthews (1980). Calculus, p.45.
http://en.wikipedia.org/wiki/Taylor's_theorem

Beautiful

30 October

S HE SINGS SILENTLY. Her face is amber and smooth, her lashes heavy as insects. She moons at the camera as though it were her lover and not a black metal lens. How does she do that? How can you ever trust her?

The thin man tries to win muscles. He looks at himself in the mirror, flexing his arms. He is skinny as a child. He can carry no weight at all. He could not even carry the amber girl's eyelashes.

The girl is achingly thin in her vest top. Her ribs stick out, her waist concaves to nothing. It's hard to imagine a child ever being there, in that inhospitable environment. It is not a growing medium. Nothing can take root.

The man pulls on a wig and smiles. His eyebrows are proud and arched as questions. He smears another mouth across his lips.

It is not heavy. He takes it well.

Dr DG Hessayon (1994). The Tree & Shrub Expert, p 51.
http://www.youtube.com/watch?v=3caZQtXaoH4

Jules Horne

And Some Interesting

31 *October*

AND SOME INTERESTING pictures appeared. They were shapely and shimmering, light and majestic, small and filigree, yet with unsayable grandeur.

They were beautiful code.

To the uninitiated, they were just numbers, arranged in sequences, looking fairly random. Some were long, extending to several pages, others were short – groups of five, six, seven – and ranked in ways that suggested a larger scheme that couldn't be discerned.

But to us, they were ineffably lovely. They flocked and grouped in weird ways. They resonated with each other, picking up each others' themes, echoing them in part, suggesting and avoiding them and creating their presence in their absence. They teased and blatantly blurted. They held such meaning in their fragile shapes – the small shapes of the digits, the larger ones of groups, the bigger hidden shape that underpinned the whole work, and could only be perceived with a mental gesture of such scope that it hurt.

And those meanings are invisible to almost everyone we meet. How to talk? How to share that awe?

Ann Jefferson (1982). *Modern Literary Theory, p* 91.
*http://www.oreilly.com/pub/wlg/*4707

Et De Sexualité

1 November

MME SANG HAD an adolescent daughter. That daughter was very beautiful, with long careless hair and even longer careless legs. Both were starting to attract increasing attention from similarly aged boys in the neighbourhood.

It was time to think about sensibilisation. Mme Sang thought hard. She couldn't keep her daughter, Cécile, in the house all the time. She couldn't fit her with a tracking device, which would be a violation of her liberté. Nor could she be on hand at every corner, popping up in cafés, appearing in shopping arcades, manifesting three rows behind in the cinema while her daughter was cosying with a new friend. They had a close relationship, but the coincidences would eventually become obvious, even to her daughter.

It was time to get the neighbours involved – une exercise de collaboration avec les ressources du milieu. There were lots of them, they all knew her daughter, and there was one on every corner, in every café and arcade, and at least one always three rows behind in the cinema. She wrote to them all, and set up Daughter Watch. Now they produce a monthly newsletter - a joyful document of young French life.

Ah! Cécile! You are so very loved.

Dominique Viart (1999). Le roman francais au XXe siècle, p.115.
http://www.sicsq.org/

Jules Horne

Smiles. He Stamps

2 November

W E REALLY FUCKING need psychiatric help. Jared is a mess. He laughs all the time. The slightest thing. A song, a word. An insect, creeping across the floor. He laughs and can't stop.

You'd think he was being tickled. But not the fun, small kind of tickling that fathers do with children. Tickle is in fact the wrong word for a gesture that renders you completely helpless, heaving, wretched. It's too soft. Sounds light, uninvasive.

No, Jared is having his guts wrenched apart by monstrous hands. It starts with a light giggle, and a look of alarm crosses his face. He knows it's about to overwhelm him, and we won't be able to talk for several days. In a few minutes he's fitting on the floor, holding his stomach together, gasping for air like a throttled fish, a hanging man, his eyes frozen open, the tears running down.

He can laugh like that for days. There is absolutely nothing in this world to laugh about. And we can all feel how it starts – with a sudden lightness, a spasm, a tremor in your gut, which travels up your chest and into a smile.

ee cummings (1960). *Selected Poems, p.31.*
http://la-folle-allure.livejournal.com/139198.html

Framed Scroll-End

3 November

MRS SAINT-JOHN FINGERS the gold lorgnette, brass inkwell, the Japanese carved figure. It's a carpenter, his saw welded to his body in yellowed ivory. He's her lucky man. He's been lucky man to her mother, and to her grandmother, and possibly beyond.

But now, somehow, the luck has turned, and he's sitting in a display case in the auction room. He'll be bought and passed on.

Most of the contents of the big scroll-end armoire are here, described as "collectables". Why did people collect collectables? And who decided what they were? It was probably just a way of making junk seem more desirable.

Now that they are all here - the gold lorgnette, the brass inkwell, the carved Japanese carpenter – they seem suddenly desirable again, in a way they hadn't been for over fifty years. She'd have raised her hand and bid for them if she could.

Judith Miller (1997). Miller's Antiques Price Guide, p. 151. http://ramsaycornish.com/documents/MicrosoftWord-28JulyWordVersion.pdf

Jules Horne

Tourist Has Largely

4 November

AFTER ONE MILLION overnight stays, the bed was getting a little tired. When Ben Frogton arrived at the hotel, with his ill-stuffed suitcase and leather gloves, and propped up at the counter, his brow sweaty with the heat of two days, Janet wasn't sure.

He was a big man. Big as a treetrunk, tall as a room. Although Room 10 was outsize, and advertised as such, it was going to struggle to cope.

"I'm not sure," she told him, and immediately regretted it.

His bulk sank, his shoulders dropped. He imploded softly into himself, collapsing his body into his bones, trying to look as small as possible.

"There's nowhere else for me to go," he said. His eyes peered out from his puffiness, wet or reflecting the light from the windows – she wasn't sure which.

In the morning, he lay on the floor, ground level, on the frayed beleaguered mattress, curled into a sluggish question-mark. The frame had collapsed, somehow silently, or sighed flat to put him at his final rest.

When they opened his suitcase, they found just one long shirt that fitted him perfectly, to well below the knee.

Julian Barnes (1995). Letters from London, p.85.
http://www.nwda.co.uk/news--events/press-releases/200601/
cumbria-tourism-praised-for-ge.aspx

An Upright Stock

5 November

HER OLD BROOM was past it. The long soughing switches had gradually fallen away, the handled tethers frayed and cracked, and the thick, knobbled handle itself, so comfortable and worn to her bony nethers, was showing signs of a resident worm.

When she picked it up a week before Halloween, a chunk fell off and rolled across the floor. It was time to put it to rest.

The new one turned out to be purple and shiny, with an upright stock and a giddying plastic smell. It had a glassy compartment in front, which could be used for storing dust or perhaps an ailing familiar. Below, it sat on rollers, and could be pushed around with a rattling ease across the wooden floor. It was easy to dust and polish.

That first night, as she rose into the air, she felt it purr beneath her with chunky satisfaction. She wondered why she'd spent so long hanging on to her spindly old broom. This new mount held her upright, like a queen, like a sidesaddle matriarch, and could warm her below on the coldest nights.

She would certainly pass the word.

RL Stevenson (1924). An Inland Voyage: Travels with a Donkey in the Cévennes, p.63. http://www.amazon.co.uk/BISSELL-3760E-Lift-Off-Cylinder-one-Metallic/dp/B000H5U3K0

Jules Horne

Everything From Chefs

6 November

FABIO FIRST BOUGHT the authentic Mexican mortar and pestle. It was a large lump of hewn mottled stone, and a nightmare to shift. He began using cumin every day in an effort to justify its existence on the counter top.

Then, no longer content with using a primitive knife, he bought a vegetable corer and peeler - a metal contraption that clamped to the table edge and whirled fully clothed apples around, stripping them bare with a finely tuned blade.

Then came the coffee grinder, and the coffee maker, and the cream frother, and the sugar spinner, the chocolate crumb dispenser, and the natty array of small biscuits to nestle in the saucers.

There wasn't enough room on the counter. He moved onto the floor:

The chopping board, the knife rack, the knife grinder, the slow cooker, the speed cooker, the freestanding electric frying pan, the griddle, the wok.

When he could no longer get to the shops, the postman brought new items to the door:

The juicer, the pulper, the mixer, the masher, the waffle iron, the sandwich toaster.

They spread into each room, stark and shiny like sculptures.

Fabio grew thin, and stood aloof in his melancholy kitchen, surrounded. Food was no longer on the menu.

Iain Sinclair (1997). Lights Out for the Territory, p.83.
http://www.chefscatalog.com/category/gifts-
by-recipient/chef-with-everything.aspx

When The Sun

7 November

WHEN THE SUN goes down, I head for the dirt track and home.

Home is round the corner, out of sight, in a clearing. I pitched it away from trees after last time. Thought they'd be good shelter. Instead, they dripped green slime trails all down the canvas. It went from looking clean and new and proud and tall to looking like some great bird had chucked on it.

I keep the fire going much as I can. Sometimes I don't get back all day and it's out. Takes a good hour to get something up again. Something I can boil water with, heat some beans.

The fire becomes your heart. It's the beat of your day. If it's still running, you've had a good day and you can lie down by it, kick back, eat and watch the shadows on your wall. If it's out, you've had a bad day and you have to fight for that little flame, talk to it, breath on it, treat it like an infant till it chooses to come good.

Today, I had a good day. The shadows are wild and loose on the walls, and the beer is cold from the stream.

David Constantine (1987). Madder, p.25.
http://www.amazon.com/When-Goes-Down-
Kenny-Chesney/dp/B00017LV7S

Jules Horne

For Each Distinct Area

8 November

For each distinct area, there are regular expressions, and more irregular ones. The regular expressions are characterised by symmetry. Certain rules are followed. You would not, for example, find two eyes on one side of the face, or a lopsided mouth, or a missing ear or limb.

The irregular expressions are characterised by asymmetry, and the following: malice, puzzlement, cruelty, insanity, fatigue, cunning, and certain other emotional states indicative of irregular thought patterns. These are to be discouraged. Paintings must follow the rules. Missing ears will be added. Eyes on different sides of the nose will be shifted. Lopsided mouths will be rectified or removed.

The artistic integrity of the paintings will of course be observed at all times.

Andrew Lane and Joyce Tait (1990). Practical Conservation, p.45.
http://www.exslt.org/set/functions/distinct/

Prepared For The Futurists

THE FIRST TIME it happened, he saw it was a coincidence. It couldn't be anything else. That he had dreamed of the fall of the Berlin Wall could be explained: he had picked images from a TV documentary, or a holiday snap, a magazine, woven them into some wishful thinking, and connected the two when it happened.

The fall of the tower at Pisa was more interesting. He couldn't recall reading or seeing anything remotely connected to it when he had the dream. It was so vivid, he could see single stones crumble from the top, watch their trajectory downward. He could replay the dream in his head.

When he saw the TV footage, he was staggered. It was the same as his dream in every respect. He was standing in the same position as the only camera. The same stone crumbled over and over in his mind.

He presumed it was a case of déjà vu. He'd seen the crash on TV, and forgotten.

When he dreamed a light aircraft crashing into the Eiffel Tower, mangling itself there like an insect, he wrote it down.

The crash happened three days later.

Then he had a dream about the London Eye. He began making phonecalls. No one listened. Not even when it exploded like a strange seedpod, its arteries on fire.

Richard Drain (1995). Twentieth Century Theatre, A Sourcebook, p.155. http://www.angelfire.com/ca/sanmateoissues/sermon13.html

Jules Horne

Mannigfachster Gestaltung

10 November

IT TAKES ALL types. Not everyone would be drawn to this kind of work. It is, after all, fairly ghoulish.

But with the help of my new book, *Essentials of Autopsy Practice*, you'll be fine. The main thing is the practice. The tricky thing is finding bodies to practice on. No longer can you just do a quick deal in a graveyard.

Instead, we work with a virtual system. The book comes with an interactive CD which you learn on. There are male and female cadavers, John and Maud. Once you've learned to carry out an autopsy on a cartoon, you'll be far better equipped to deal with the real world. John and Maud are wonderfully realised complete human beings, based on real cadavers.

Their tissue responds exactly as you'd expect, and the level of skin tone, hair and blood vessel detail is astounding. Many of our trainee autopsy practitioners report feeling nauseous when they cut Maud's yellow chest open.

This we consider a success.

Friedrich Engels (Dietz, 1951).Dialektik der Natur, p.183.
http://www.springerlink.com/content/h65t211p8234l532/

Gulliver Press

E MAIL TO A young poet:
When you go to a reading, make sure you're decked out in literary apparel, so that other poets recognise you.

That may include an attention-getting t-shirt with an obscure quote that one other person might recognise. We can supply t-shirts which have already been fully field-tested. We guarantee that you will be assured intrigue and chest-glances, and that everyone will go home and look up the words, and spend sleepless nights if they don't find them. (Our bespoke products feature specially crafted aphorisms – one-offs which no one will ever trace. This will cause confusion, frustration, depression, sleepless nights and ultimately admiration, which we consider good value for the price).

The other thing we can supply is a haunted, faraway expression. These are available in male and female versions in several different sizes, ranging from junior (adolescent) to grandee (senescent). Wear one and stand against a prominent wall. We guarantee - you will not go unnoticed.

Eugen Gomringer (1972). konkrete poesie, p.75.
http://www.cafepress.com/gulliver

Jules Horne

Cailles Replètes

12 November

B ARBARIC POEMS, WHERE the fat quails sing
Their quailish songs and lay their speckled eggs,
Where syllables dance and staunchly refuse to conform
With any laid-down versifier's laws,
Where words erupt and wear their meanings large
And spreading wild beyond the corset-line,
Where words have beards and smoke illicit drugs
That draw deep down into the throat of truth,
Where words cut ice and slice through sense and time,
Where words engulf the world and nail our breath,
Which cut me short when seconds tick to nil.

Christian Damour (1973). *Leconte de Lisle, p.49.*
http://fr.wikipedia.org/wiki/Ravine_Saint-Gilles

I Read Recently

13 November

I READ RECENTLY. IT was though an axe had been taken to
my head. For the first time in years, it was split wide open,
gaping horribly, with the cold air nipping at the innards in a
way that made them shrivel. You can take a metaphor too far.

But with my head gaped open in that bloody way, I walked
around in a daze. The world looked different. The colours
were scoured fresher, the dirts far dustier. The people looked
strange: their eyes sharper, darting, fearful, their bodies twisting and ducking against the invisible forces that swirled
around them. They walked not upright, but as though pushed,
and pulled, and pressured and swayed – and as though they
didn't know where they were going.

With my axe-opened head and my metaphor, I felt new. I
straightened my shoulders and walked and watched. I knew
where I was going, though not my destination.

Carol Shields (2002). *Unless, p.51.*
http://bocktherobber.com/2007/10/things-i-read-recently

Jules Horne

Entrancement

Look into my eyes. Look into my eyes. Watch the pulsing light. Drift.

In a moment you will wake up refreshed and content. But first, I want you to take all your clothes off. Yes, that, too. And that. It is warm and relaxing in the room. You are perfectly comfortable.

And now I want you to stand with your legs apart. That's it. Relaxed and comfortable, with your legs apart.

And now twist your upper body round to the right, and look back at me over your shoulder. That's right. Further. Further. Relaxed and comfortable.

And now drop your head and look up at me with a submissive expression, your eyes large and inviting, while running your tongue across your lips. That's right. Good. Relaxed and comfortable.

And now take your right hand and stroke your pussy, while squeezing your nipple with your left. No, you may not untwist your upper body, nor stop running your tongue across your lips. Relaxed and comfortable. I said relaxed and comfortable, comfortable and relaxed. You are enjoying the feel of your right hand stroking your pussy.

And now take your right middle finger and –

Oh, for goodness' sake, get up! What do you mean, you can't balance? Have you never seen heels before?

George Bruce (1991). *The Land Out There, p.55.*
http://entrancement.co.uk/

Latin Word

KEENNESS, AND BATTLEFIELD. There's a Latin word which covers both. Acies.

There's a word which means orange, and level crossing, in a forgotten Creole of South America. Another which means friendship and cuttlefish in a lost Finno-Ugric tongue. We take different realities and in some world or other, some culture already past or still to be, they are the same. Language converges them, cogs them together, and they vibrate in tandem, somewhere between themselves and each other. That is how metaphors work: by creating a bridge between two words and dropping our brains in the middle, where they fight. Our imaginations flourish in that bottomless space. Our pictures live. Like and unlike always share something, even if it's only the thought you've just bound them with.

Jean Aitchison (1978). Teach Yourself Linguistics, p.55.
http://www.math.ubc.ca/~cass/frivs/latin/latin-dict-full.html

Jules Horne

Machine May Be

16 November

THE LEECHES WERE edgy. Suck this for a malarkey, said one. Not good, not good, said another, lazily bloating on an old man's chest.

We'll have to unionise, said another. Elect a leader. Pool our resources.

I can't take any more, said a shiny young leech which had overdosed on a big girl's belly and was having trouble digesting the consequences.

It's inevitable, said an old, gnarled leech with blunt teeth. It's progress. We have to roll with it. We can't fight them. This thing is bigger than us.

The apothecary hurdled in the bright new machine, its pronged suction cups waving in the air.

It looked hungry. It looked thin. It had 5,000 litres of capacity and a row of twenty patients. They stirred in their drugged sleep. They wouldn't see the morning.

Dorothea Brande (1934). Becoming a Writer, p.65. http://news. nationalgeographic.com/news/2001/12/1219_wireleeches.html

A La Résidence

17 November

You'll find the French way of life infectious. You'll find yourself driving on the right, learning what signs mean despite yourself. You'll find yourself shopping in markets where fresh fish is sold, and eating goat's cheese.

You'll find yourself starting to say "oui" and "non" and other words associated with everyday life in France. These might include "bonjour" and "ça va" and the words that appeared in school textbooks. Words you took great pains never to remember and have in the interim completely forgotten.

You'll find yourself absorbing clichés: scarves, if you're a woman; lovers if you're a man. Or at the very least, the idea of lovers. This could pose a threat to your longstanding relationship with Eric, or Irene, your recently retired spouse, with whose help you bought the retirement cottage.

You may find yourself having long afternoons, wandering the countryside, or learning to shoot. You may find yourself avoiding other Brits, who are embarrassing and ungainly in brogues.

Now is probably a good time to reconsider your purchase.

Pierre Benoit (1924). La Chatelaine du Liban, p.89.
http://www.laresidence.co.uk/

How Do You Say "Well"?

18 November

I T'S TIME TO find the sound that best supports your message. You may think that sound is a word. Something like "peace", perhaps. Or "rebel". Or "I'm alive".

The problem with words is that they are too slippery. "Peace" sounds like "piece". "Rebel" is vague and will quickly deflate. "I'm alive" is a little circular, a little Descartes.

We, on the other hand, specialise in sounds. Sounds are universal. They don't need translation. They are individual and varied, yet can be heard and understood by everyone from the very young to the very old.

Aggggh, for example, is a rich stew of frustration and anguish. It contains tension, duration and release. It requires no unnecessary activation of the tongue. It's universal. Primal.

Aggggh may not support your eventual message. But I'd like you to try it now, here, among friends. It'll give you a flavour of what we do.

Vaclav Havel (1992). Selected Plays, p.103.
http://www.sayitwell.com/

Two Payroll Bandits

19 November

S LY AND FANNER died instantly: Sly slumped over the door of the safe, and Fanner on the floor, legs straight and arms round his head, as though lying like a good boy would save him.

There were five of them. From the corner of his eye, Sly had caught someone pass the corridor window as they wound up their late-night meeting. Thought it was the cleaner, Joe. If he'd thought about it longer than an instant, he'd have realised the hurrying shadow was a whole foot taller than Joe, but that instant brought the man pointing round the door with a shotgun.

Sly wondered about the shotgun – why such a large weapon? What would it do in that tight, hot space? But that thought, too, was over fast, and he was suddenly flung against the wall, his cheek flattened to the scratchy flock, and his keys ripped from his trouser pocket.

Where was Fanner? Fanner was out there. He'd be back from the john shortly and walk straight into this mess. Or he'd see the five men waiting, and turn and run for his life.

Tom Bryan (1997). Rich Man, Beggar Man, Indian Chief, p.49.
http://query.nytimes.com/gst/abstract.html?res=9902E6D9143CE5
33A25752C0A9679C946095D6CF

Jules Horne

But I Assume

20 November

ASSUME NOTHING, PRESUME nothing. There I go, exhorting again. I wonder what that need is? Why the need to teach, guide, prod in certain directions?

It's not as if I've got it all sorted myself.

Here I sit, surrounded by paper and chaos, trying to carve a path through life, in my head and in reality.

This certainly isn't ideal. Most people seem to have things far better sussed, nailed, organised. They know where they're heading and how to head there.

Whereas I'm guided by the words my fingers find in books, and the books my hands find in a blind walk from the room, and the stories my head finds milling in five minutes of attention to itself.

It's not a very practical, concrete, helpful way of approaching life. I'm letting everything else guide me – the given roads, the preordained paths, the grooved instincts, the rutted routines, and the riffs and expectations of my head.

Which is why I exhort so much. Not for you, but for me.

Frank Kuppner (1994). Something Very Like Murder, p.239.
http://sdk.typepad.com/trust/2005/05/assume_nothing_.html

Elastic Waists

2 1 November

S TAN WAS GROWING. He did his best to hide his expanding waist beneath baggier t-shirts, larger jackets, bigger belts. It did no good.

It was happening very fast. He just needed to look at food to put on weight. That's what he told his wife, Jocelyn. She thought it was just a phrase, but it was true.

His world was full of pictures of food – chicken dinner adverts, meringue recipes, moving conveyor belts of sodapop, burgers, beer on the telly every night. There were hoardings on every street corner, and coloured menus in every bar.

Every time he spotted something edible, even from the corner of his eye, his body lurched. He felt the calories sucked into his flesh with a slight tug. They coursed round his body, settling mostly around his waist.

He tried shutting his eyes. He tried not eating.

Still the calories came. They tucked themselves into all the hollow spaces, and filled out his liver.

First, the doctor has to believe him.

Roddy Doyle (1990). The Snapper, p.77. http://shopping.msn. com/results/mens-socks-underwear/bcatid6778/target/12-70/ forsale?text=category:mens-socks-underwear+Seller:Target

Obstructive

22 *November*

O CH, THERE IS no cure. Get over it. You'll decline, fail, wither, decrepe. And there's nothing you can do.

In the meantime, there are parties. Get out there. Drink. Eat cocktail things on tables. Talk to people who won't talk back. Drink again. Eat the dregs of cocktail things. Talk to people under the table. Dance.

We're all together in this multisome reel. There are steps and shapes and configurations. You don't need to know them all. You don't even need to recognise them when they hit you in the gullet. You only need to be pulled along, by a stranger hand, or find yourself whirled into their midst, and jig or trip or slide. It'll all be over and you'll all go home.

Under the table, crumbs are lurking. Pick them up for sustenance. Cheddar and onion, olive and radicchio. Bread, and bread, and bread.

Eat, for the whirl will soon be over.

Richard Mabey (1980). *The Common Ground, p.83. http://www.nlm. nih.gov/medlineplus/copdchronicobstructivepulmonarydisease.html*

Removed

23 November

THE TOWN WAS in need of a face lift. Nobody went there. It was grey and grim, with rain-soaked paving and windowless walls.

There was also the matter of the bird. It roosted in the town square, big as a building, and caused a major obstruction.

Its eggs were the size of prams, its feathers as big as doors. It cawed when it was content, snuggling into its clutch of five, and shrieked when anyone came too near. No matter that the townsfolk only came up to its knee – they were still a threat to the future of its incubating brood.

Experts were sought. They listened and hummed and thought about the problem. It was decided that the bird couldn't be forced to leave. It would have to go of its own volition.

Ernst the trombonist is now practising a mating call. He's trying to sound like a twenty-foot bird so horny that eggs seem a boring irrelevance.

Let's leave him in peace.

Laurie Campbell (1996). *Golden Eagles, p.22.*
http://news.bbc.co.uk/1/hi/england/beds/bucks/herts/4774660.stm

Jules Horne

Lumpy Before

24 November

It's never been lumpy before. I've made this recipe every year for fifty years. Ever since I was in my twenties. Every summer, I buy the oranges, get out the mincer, peel and chop and boil it up in the jelly pan.

The air in the kitchen is sticky. My lips taste of oranges. My hair curls with sugar. The steam rises from the pan and I stand for hours, skimming off the bubbling scum.

But this year, something didn't work. Was it too much sugar? Not enough water? I tried thinning down, I tried boiling for longer. Great lumps were forming in the marmalade, big as tennis balls, and welling up again whenever I broke them down. I stirred and stirred, reducing the heat, but still they formed.

It was impossible to pour the unset jam into the jars. The lumps were too big for the necks. I sat with the cooling pan. They solidified slowly, and I ate them one by one.

Marlis Weber (1987). The Single Vegetarian, p.65.
http://www.scribd.com/doc/192409/jams-and-jelly-recipes

The Opposite

25 November

S o HE WENT out of the door and turned left, heading for god knows where. He'd never been there before.

Round the corner, the street ran out. The quiet suburb he'd been living in all those years simply ended. There were no trees, no buildings but the backs of those he'd just left behind. Ahead was a concrete arena that stretched as far as he could see.

He started walking.

There was nothing to interrupt the horizon. The sun was lowering towards the edge of the world, reddening as it went. He looked back at the shrinking street, the backs of the houses he knew. His shadow stretched long across the slabs, his head folded at the neck onto the nearest building.

He walked still further and turned.

His head had left the building. His legs were giant's legs, unencumbered and strong.

He strode out towards the falling sun. There was a dot ahead, moving away.

He turned left again, and followed.

Plato (Penguin, 1953). The Republic, p.193. http://www.tv.com/ seinfeld/the-opposite/episode/2326/summary.html

Jules Horne

Full In 'Er Face

26 November

THEY MADE A feature film. It was terrible: a schlocky, violent affair among friends who were no longer friends once the movie was over.

There was a lot of waiting around in the rain. A lot of empty stomachs and tired sandwiches. A lot of late nights in the bar trying to rekindle the excitement.

The leading actors fell out over closeups. She was all for them, and he would have none, being self-conscious about pock scarring from his teens. It made the viewpoint skewed. The film now focused in on her, and left him on the margins. This was contrary to the script and the story.

Now the camera followed her close – her every blink and eyelash, her every breath and moue.

He was an adjunct. His poster credits were shrunk to a smaller font. On the screen, his name flew past in half a second.

When he saw the film, he realised his moment had passed without trace.

They never spoke again.

Simon Armitage (2006). *Tyrannosaurus Rex versus the Corduroy Kid, p.29. http://akas.imdb.com/title/tt0494129/fullcredits*

Zu Können!

27 November

CLICK ON "WEITER". This will take you to the next stage, where more is possible. Hang-gliding, gourmet cooking, acrobatic gurning with your lips stretched around your ears.

You only need to believe.

And then on: space travel, extreme knitting, sex with the outermost recesses of your mind. It's all possible.

On and on. On and in and further. Strain and strive and reach and–

Universes to visit in a weekend. Peace to provide for a world and its neighbour. Slit a door through into a parallel place and return in time for tea.

Go there. Out with you. Head ahead. Weiter. Weiter so.

When you get to the end, you may want to stop and look back. Resist.

It will only fill you with dread.

On and on. Weiter so. It'll all end in tears.

Hermann Hesse (1952). Klingsors letzter Sommer, p.73.
http://www.adobe.com/de/products/acrobat/readstep2.html

Jules Horne

Pour Se Libérer

S HE FLICKED THE lighter and held the fag to her lips. It tasted dry and cottony. She lit it and sucked gratefully, her nose and throat filling.

It was the last one. Yet again, the last one. She breathed the leather aroma round her chest, the warmth reaching deep into her gut, her nerves.

She felt calm. It would work. This time, it would work.

There were five fags left in the packet. She wasn't going to smoke them – five o'clock was the cut-off. But it seemed a shame to waste them.

A man was passing – bent, hurried, heading for the bus.

Hey, she called. Want some fags?

He looked at her, puzzled.

I've given up. Just this minute. As of now.

Oh, he said. Yeah.

She handed him the packet.

Sure? he said.

No, she said, without a smile.

She kicked the half-finished end of her final fag onto the pavement and toed it dead.

He checked the packet, tucking it shut. As it disappeared into his jacket pocket, she almost put her hand.

Thanks, he shrugged.

Before he had turned the corner, she was already missing something.

Michel Tournier (1972). Vendredi ou les limbes du Pacifique, p.143.
http://www.jarrete.qc.ca/

In My Room?

29 November

H is room was his whole world. The floorboards were tectonic plates, the carpets and rugs above were layers of grass and moss, threadbare here and there.

On the floor were mountains of books, stacked precariously. Sometimes there were landslides and everything collapsed onto itself. And he built them up again, more neatly, small on top of large.

Spiders crawled in the undergrowth, especially in summer. He watched them disappear into crevices and potholes down below.

His seat was a throne, on which he sat, above it all, swivelling. The light shone with daylight colours and switched to night at night.

He rarely needed to leave. He had everything he wanted. Food came to his door.

He read, and listened to loud, crashing tracks to kill the voices in his head. Voices that told him about the world he was god of, with the floorboards his tectonic plates, and the grass and moss threadbare below.

Ali Smith (2005). The Accidental, p.105.
http://en.wikipedia.org/wiki/In_My_Room_(song)

Jules Horne

Generation Has

Mᴏʀᴇ ᴛᴏ ʟᴏsᴇ. The younger generation has more to lose. More life in front of it. More to cut short if it ends when it shouldn't.

There's a dwindling supply and we can't see the end of it. It soughs past and past. Hurtles, sometimes. There are days when you wake up and go to sleep and remember nothing between.

There are days when you want to grab it and haul it to a standstill. Like Superman. Or one of the heroes. The one who seized the world and turned it backwards. He was wearing something stretchy. He had muscles the size of goats.

It's all a blur. And the blur doesn't slow down. No – it gets faster. When I write the manual, I'll tell them that. Everything that seems so full of potential is actually all there is. Taste it as it passes. Breathe it in.

You have more to lose and yet you waste it all. With age comes parsimony and want.

Thomas Paine (Wordsworth, 1996). Rights of Man, p.85.
http://www.newscientist.com/article/dn11741.html

Excise In

IT WAS BAD news. On thick, glossy paper, the government was telling him that he owed them £3,000. There was no way he could pay.

He thought of the thick, glossy paper, and the way the government had sent such bad news on such an expensive substrate. How many trees had been felled, to be grated into that rich-smelling parchment? How much bleach had been expended to turn it white, and how much dye tipped to turn it such a tasteful shade of vellum?

Why was such a large font used? Surely they could halve their paper bills by printing in 8-point. They could halve them still further by printing on both sides, and sending two bills in one envelope – one for next-door, perhaps, who usually got her tax bill at the same time of year.

And then there was the person who composed the letter, and printed it, and folded into three, and inserted it into an envelope. Surely savings could be made there? And since the nation was ultimately reaping the benefit, surely the queen could give permission to forgo the use of stamps?

He worked out that the potential saving was £2,999. The remaining pound he would pay. It was strict but fair. The government would learn to be less cavalier in future.

Nicholas Roe (1999). A Guide to a Freelance Lifestyle.
http://www.hmrc.gov.uk/

Jules Horne

It Was Remembering

2 *December*

IT WAS THE last thrash of empire. Britain was dying as a force in the world. It knew it, and didn't – those two thoughts held together, fighting each other out.

It decided to lash out one final time. Because it could. It knew how. It had the people, the machines, the strategies, the structures that allowed such things to proceed.

Orders were given. Strength was summoned into all the corners that together make up a country: politics, economics, media, logistics. The land sent out a tongue of itself into another, and lashed as well as it remembered.

There was no point. This was somewhere known, in the deep recesses that together make up a country: minds, brains, hearts, convictions. The country lashed, failed and was quiet.

There were aftershocks, fewer and fewer, for a long while. For centuries.

Ian McEwan (1998). Amsterdam, p.67.
http://news.bbc.co.uk/1/hi/world/middle_east/5199392.stm

Rein Gar Nichts

3 December

S WEET FANNY ADAMS, in her mob cap and corset, straddling the bedhead like an adventurous horse.

All of her judders as she bounces up and down: her glorious creamy breasts welling sumptuously from her bodice, her dimpling thighs and their fleshy expanses, her tautened arms clung fiercely to the post. And above it all, her jumping curls, sprung from her cap, spilling sweatily across her brow, up and down, left and right, to and fro.

Let me stroke them to the side, sweet Fanny Adams! Let me mess them royally with both buried hands. Let me coil them round my fingers and pull you in towards me.

Sweet Fanny! Sweet woman! Sweet nothing and all!

Max Frisch (1963). Biedermann und die Brandstifter, p.49.
http://www.dict.cc/deutsch-englisch/rein+gar+nichts.html

Jules Horne

Wenn Ich Übertreibe

4 December

WHEN I EXAGGERATE, I really push the boat out. It's a colossal boat, too - absolutely huge. Takes ten of us to push us out. On a good day. On a bad day, it takes thousands.

It's an ocean liner. Crew of 2,000 and berths for a small town population of 16,000. Or, depending on how you count, a city of 250,000. That means it's pretty crowded. You can't move for people and their gins and tonics, all rowed on the decks for what seems like miles, and probably is.

They're crammed into their berths, six to a bed, and have to sleep in shifts, playing poker or sunbathing on pre-booked chairs the rest of the time. Whole families have been born here, died and been buried at sea. Whole generations. It's a dynastic business, this boat. Most of them have never met anyone from outside, on the land. They sail from country to country and terrorise the landlubbers whenever they draw near.

And I've only told you the half of it.

Ingo Schulze (1998). Simple Storys, p.93.
http://www.wer-weiss-was.de/theme143/article2883564.html

Knew My Name

SING-A-LONG-A-SINGSONG: NO ONE knew my name.
I turned up at my birth and no one had heard of me.
Said my mother: Who he?
Said my father: Search me.
They looked at me blankly and scratched their heads.
They turned me once over, went back to their beds.
I lay semi-drowned in a puddle of tears
Trying out words for size and fit:
How bout his? How bout hers?
How bout this? How bout theirs?
Is it thus? Is it these? Is it that? Is this it?
I'm still looking
For the place
Where somebody knows
So I can settle
Grow moss
On the ends of my toes.
One day I'll know.
Until then I'll go
Sing-a-long-a-singsong.
All together now.

Ursula Le Guin (1973). *Earthsea Trilogy, p.*107.
http://www.lyricsmania.com/lyrics/marc_broussard_lyrics_3011/
lyrics_9069/no_one_knew_my_name_lyrics_104744.html

Jules Horne

Offer No Satisfactory Explanation...

6 December

...for the human mind. It can't help it. It does what it does, especially late at night.

You can wheel out dreams and dissect them, or look at thoughts as they whirr around like gnats, seeing them form and fade, emerge and die. You can dredge up memories and pick them apart, in all their unreliable glory, their pointed stories shoring up your every habit and decision.

It will do no good. Your mind is always in flux. You can feed it daily, and it'll absorb all you throw at it. Out in the landscape, you can head it towards the fringed silhouettes of trees, or the damp grass underfoot, or the coolness of air on your cheek, the near and far, the hand and head, the every possible nuance of your perception. You'll never monitor all of them.

You'll see what you choose to see, and be imprisoned by it. So is it too much to ask you to choose carefully? Choose widely, wildly, wisely and never trust a fragment.

Michel Faber (ed) (2001). Shorts 4, p.69.
http://www.planetpapers.com/Assets/4917.php

Would Do Me Good

7 December

I WOULD DO ME. I frequently do.
That aside, what's not to love? Smooth green skin, perfect quarter-inch moles, round as coins, and a tail as proud and curved as a ship's prow.

I would do me good, in fact.

My teeth are pretty good: two white rows, only the occasional passing place from encounters with bigger, hairier monsters. I like to think the gaps are cute – they suggest a history, a flaw. Something to pull the bigger-hearted.

I only have three arms. I used to get hung up about that, but not any more. I love it. It makes me unique, interesting. Gives me stories to tell. How I got that way. How my four parents' fervent mating went awry and gave an interesting new spin on the species. The ones who can't get over that – tough. Their loss. They'll never know what I can do with three arms. One, and two, and ... oh boy.

You have my number. Give me a call.

Alan Wilkins (2004). *The Nest, p.25.*
http://www.prankplace.com/tshirts_iwoulddome.htm

Jules Horne

High Street, Oxford

8 December

H ENRY TAUNT WAS a photographer. He sometimes
wondered how he'd have turned out if he'd had another
name, like Henry Joy or Henry Encourage, but thanks to his
father, that wasn't the case.

People queued up to have their portrait taken. Henry's
style was unusual. He'd offer them a seat, then, just as they
were about to sit down, pull it away. They'd fall on the ground,
in an ungainly and often painful fashion: CLICK!

He'd look at their clothes (which we know as Victorian)
and point and laugh: "What a ridiculous hat! How can you
possibly wear a black tube on your head all day long? What is
it for, apart from making you slightly taller?" And their faces
would grow red, and purple, and puce, and their cheeks puff
like bloater fish, and he'd grab his picture: CLICK!

And he'd make fun of their cover ups: "You may look all
right on the outside, with your lace and swishy fabrics, but
inside, your corset is fraying apart." And while their eyebrows
were knitting together in a furious frown: CLICK!

His photos of gurning, flailing, blurred individuals were
a great hit with fellow photographers when they held their
annual outtake parties. Just not with his clients. He was a
century before his time.

Oxford University Press (1981).
University of Oxford Examination Decrees & Regulations, p.375.
http://en.wikipedia.org/wiki/High_Street,_Oxford

Lebzeiten

9 December

S CHILLER WAS A working playwright. Plays were written, handed out, tried out, played out, revised, ditched, improved, edited and mangled around to their general benefit by a vast array of performers, directors, musicians, set designers, costume designers, props people and theatre managers, not forgetting the audience members, whose response to the play at certain moments didn't meet expectations, so the script had to be changed.

When it came to publishing Schiller's work, there was a problem. He wanted it to look grand, complete and timeless, like Shakespeare's portfolios. He wanted it to look as though it had always been that way, and had only ever appeared in that perfect form, all gorgeous typography and perfect words in as near as dammit the right order.

The printer sweated blood. "What do you want, Herr Schiller? Was wollt Er?"

He couldn't get it right. There was always some tweak or tinker that needed to be added, mostly after a new performance, when Herr Schiller happened to sit in the audience and get a new idea.

In the end, the printer had to pull rank. "Publish and be damned," he said. He didn't even pass on the proofs. The plays would have to stand as they were, in their inky, perilous state.

And yet we read them as though they're dead.

Eduard Petiška (1994). Sagenschatz der böhmischen Burgen, p. 103.
http://www.ingentaconnect.com/content/rodopi/
abng/2006/00000061/00000001/art00005

Jules Horne

Gates Of Hell

10 December

THE FIGURES WERE escaping from the bronze. The people writhed and screamed as the melted metal stiffened and trapped them. Their arms flung wide, they tried to escape the hardening, but their toes were already dipped and caught. The bronze crept up their shins and to their thighs, up their torsos and to their arms, along every tightening inch of their hands, their fingers, which still clawed towards the air, until they were dead.

Only the Thinker sat still above it all, letting the metal claim him slow bit by bit.

The pair of the Kiss managed to escape before it was too late. Only some of her long hair was caught, combed into bronze, and was torn away by his hand.

It's still there, coiled forever into the gates. The lovers ran free and grew old somewhere.

Bernard Champigneulle (1967). *Rodin, p.91.*
http://en.wikipedia.org/wiki/The_Gates_of_Hell

Leaves And A Saw-Toothed Notching

11 December

IT'S BRISTLY, UNPLEASANT and stinging. It's also extremely varied in its morphology.

Since vats of yellow chemicals escaped from the industrial buildings on the banks of the river Tweed, it's been changing fast.

In the old days, nettles used to look like nettles. Now, they're putting out wide, leafy canopies and impersonating rhubarb. Some of them are digging deep into the soil, thickening up their roots and producing gentle, frondy growths just above ground level. They can easily be mistaken for carrots. Some are even going perennial – you can see thickets, sometimes two-foot trunks, and branches above, with blossom in the spring and a sprinkle of what looks uncannily like Boscop apples. And then there are the nettles that have mastered the art of potato simulation – usually Pink Fir, or something knobbly, and which even manage the pretence of blight to put growers off the scent.

There are no guarantees any more. The only way to work out what's what is to look at the molecular structure. Until then, we'll carry on being stung, and stung, and stung.

Kenneth A Beckett (1999). Growing Under Glass, p.67.
http://www.oardc.ohio-state.edu/weedguide/
singlerecord.asp?id=210

Jules Horne

Once And For All

12 December

HIS PHOTOS PROVE once and for all that UFOs exist. They show large, metallic, cigar-shaped objects hovering over his house, sending streamers of light down his chimney. The objects have windows through which can be seen grey figures that would seem to be peering out, if they had discernible eyes. Each ship – if that's what they are – has a jet stream below offering some kind of propulsion, and a light haze of steam fills the night air around one end, which appears to be a kind of gas exchanger.

These craft were so emphatically not clouds that I'm surprised you even raise the question. Johnson was standing out in his garden with a group of neighbours – around twelve, I'm led to believe – and all have similar photos in their camera. We've printed them all up, pinned them to the incident board, and you can see a perfect semicircle of spaceships, all from the slightly different angles where the neighbours stood, some a little shaky, as though the hands were trembling.

As, indeed, they probably were. Johnson has all the proof we could wish for. And still we don't believe.

Chris Baines (1986). The Wild Side of Town, p.45.
http://idioms.thefreedictionary.com/once+for+all

Lowdown

13 December

I, LIKE THE fool on the hill, am waiting for her to catch up. She has a basket full of washing on her head, sleeves dragging out of it, green and striped. Her belly's full and round. Thinks I can't see it. Shrugs off the weight of it. Her skirt is too short, rides up at the front to take the swell. She's picking her nails, flicking out peel and pith from where she's made the lunch.

My own bundle is tight-wrapped and solid. No sleeves flapping anywhere. Nothing able to escape. It's like a rock on my head. I feel its motion as I walk, like a deciding wave, somewhere between fall and move, move and fall.

She smiles as she strides up the hill. I find myself wishing I could stride as loudly as that, the sleeves in my bundle hanging.

James Smart (2003). *The List Bar Guide To Edinburgh & Glasgow, p.63.*
http://www.lowdown.co.zm/

Jules Horne

Macht Keinen Unterschied

Herr Kirsch and Frau Kirsch-Cunningham were separating. There were two children, Norbert and Michael. The fairest way was clearly to separate the children, too, and allow the parents to take one each. Norbert and Michael weren't happy. Their father was much wealthier, and likely to take them on foreign holidays and buy them electronics. Their mother hadn't worked since bringing them into the world, and had laid aside her law degree to the detriment of her mental abilities and self-esteem. As a result, she was depressed, and prone to weeping.

They decided to take it in turns – Norbert one month, and Michael the next – parent by parent. Christmas would be divided up more finely on a day to day basis. Both parent had extra rooms for them to stay in, and extra sets of bedclothes and crockery. No one felt entirely responsible – Herr Kirsch resentful that his ex-wife hadn't shouldered the entire caring burden, and Frau (now) Cunningham that her ex-husband had become wealthy at her expense.

Someone knocked at the door, and disturbed the end of this story. Sorry. It probably doesn't make much difference to Norbert's eventual fate.

Rudolf Bussmann (1998). Über Erwarten, p.101.
http://www.ra-cunningham.de/rechtsanwalt-familienrecht-
nuernberg/neues-unterhaltsrecht-2007.htm

Materials. Margaret Copy

MARGARET SIGHED AT the tower of paper on her desk. She would never get through it. Not in a lifetime. Sometimes she wanted to stuff it all into a rubbish bag and start again – declare bankruptcy on the bureaucracy that was claiming her life. Or start a fire. That would do. Strike a match and tickle it to the ends of a single sheet of paper, coquettishly, giving it the choice. And then run like (yes) blazes.

Proposition 36 would have to be gutted. It wasn't enough just to tweak here and there, modify some of its more stringent sentiments with an "as appropriate" or "in certain circumstances" or even just "mostly", "usually", or "typically". No, it would have to be filleted completely. She would have to revisit all the precedents, carve them apart, drain out their essences and make something entirely new.

This would be a lifetime's work, and one which would go completely unnoticed. Lawyers, officials, councillors and counsellors would base whole careers on her single perfect paragraph. Its very perfection was its complete invisibility.

She sighed. It was much more rewarding to do a terrible job. At least you were noticed.

Michael Mail (2002). *Coralena, p.95.*
http://www.drugpolicy.org/library/staffwritten/dooley.cfm

Jules Horne

Quid Tum Si Fuscus Amyntas

17 December

So WHAT? IF I kick the coffee pot? What then? If I jump from the window.

I can do what I want.

I'm in that waiting place, between doing and not doing. It's on the tip of me, whether to stretch out my leg and knock the whole thing over. Whether to open my eyes, put my book aside, and clamber over the sill.

On the tip of me, and either could be or. This way and that way, and - while waiting - in between.

In between is the gloriousest feeling. Choices, choices. And what small weight arrives to tip me one way or the other? How much does a decision weigh? How much an impulse? What do I feel first, and second, and for and againstly?

I'm weighing up my thoughts. Maybe I should open my eyes? What then?

André Gide (Folio, 1987). Les nourritures terrestres, p.131.
http://www.dappledthings.org/mqa07/artprose01.php

Am Markt Im Freien

18 December

VICES ARE NOT crimes. Johnny knew he could drink as much as he wanted. Nobody was going to stop him. Plenty had tried.

He stotted across the market place, fixing one flower barrel and then the next. The cobbles were wet. His soles kept slipping. He landed at each barrel and grasped it, steadying himself, then lunged out carefully towards the next.

He was going to be in trouble. Trouble again. Always trouble. And he could so easily keep himself out of it if he chose. That's what his wife said, his daughters. And he agreed each time: next time, I'll know. Next time, I won't.

And this was another next time, as he stood by a flower barrel and focused on the one behind. Geraniums. Or something red. Some kind of flower.

A Russon (1965). Advanced German Course - Key, p.39.
http://www.derfreiemarkt.ch/

Jules Horne

Bunny's Enthusiasm

19 December-

CERTAINLY OUR NEW ally had a ramshackle look. Bunny was tall, and stooped at every conceivable angle: the shoulders, the waist, the elbows, the knees. His hair hung flat on his bony head, and his jackets and shirts were worn at the cuff.

And yet he spoke like God's own angel.

His voice was quiet, authoritative, with the spit and polish of a long, expensive education. His vowels sang out as though they came from unstopped pipes in mediaeval chapel organs. When he spoke, he was choral, as nobody could ever disagree with him. He was the voice of truth, of establishment, of money.

He never spoke a word of sense that anyone could remember. But it didn't matter. He soughed up and down, like a melodic willow, and somehow made a tremendous impression.

That he could be a spy had never crossed our minds.

Janette Winterson (1985). Boating for Beginners, p.77.
http://books.google.com/books?id=x2SIhYoBBb4C&pg=PA78
&lpg=PA78&dq=bunny's+enthusiasm&source=web
&ots=Zg61PUax9W&sig=IhkSBW25ErysfSyT0KYJYh1Jhvs

The Youngest Daughter

20 December

THE YOUNGEST DAUGHTER confronted the troll. It was a great slobbering thing, giving off a powerful stench of curdled milk and sour fish in brine.

"Go back to where you came from," she said. "You won't fit in here. The people will never accept you.

The troll shifted in an agitated manner, its ears reddening.

"I've nowhere else to go."

"You've the whole world," the youngest daughter insisted.

"That's what I thought," said the troll. "But I've tried everywhere. It's always the same reaction. People just don't like what they see."

"Maybe if you smartened up?" said the youngest daughter. "Bit of a haircut, maybe a bath?"

"Tried that," said the troll. "If you lived in my kind of hole, you wouldn't be able to keep it up for long, either."

He looked at the daughter, blinking his great leathery eyelids.

"Are people really that superficial?"

The daughter nodded.

The troll turned away and trudged on to a far new hole, on the hiddenest side of the wood, where he began to write his memoirs.

Miles Krasse (1976). O'Neill's Music of Ireland, p.99.
http://en.wikipedia.org/wiki/Youngest_son

Jules Horne

Made You Want

LEOPARD JUST WORKS. All day, he's on the phone, moving things on, clinching deals, making sure the shipments of logistics have arrived at their proper destinations in good time.

It's a full-time job. That's how it was advertised in the Middle Management Gazette. "Full-Time Appointment", it said, quite clearly. Why so many people failed to grasp that is unclear. Some of them expected holidays, weekends and even nights to be free.

You soon put them right on that.

"Here's what you signed," you said, waving the contract under their bloodshot eyes. Usually, they read their names through a blur of tears. And then they turned back to the phone, and wearily heaved the receiver to their ears. By and large, they disappeared soon after.

Leopard was different. You knew that, the moment he arrived. He had an air of challenge about him. "Full-time means full-time," he nodded, and rubbed his hands together, smiling straight at you. "That goes without saying."

You looked away. There was something strange about him. Something about the too-pressed cut of his jacket.

You couldn't know that he'd still be here, all and every night, weekends and holidays, some five years later, still wearing that same too-pressed jacket. He made you want to cry, but you still can't work out why.

CS Lewis (1954). *The Horse and his Boy, p.117.*
http://www.apple.com/getamac/

Je Me Suis Embarqué

22 December

I EMBARKED ON A dancing ship
the supple waves taught me cadences
more beautiful than human song
my feet forgot the ground
I rolled with the tides forgot the flat
moving on a swell a roll a surge a break
all motion all current all well and wane
all undertow and overturn
above it all on the galloping line
where sea meets air in white suspend
breath meets salt and gasp meets sing
concertina froth and triplet tide
I danced to the jig of the sea

Nathalie Sarraute (1953). Martereau, p.145.
http://www.recmusic.org/lieder/get_text.html?TextId=11467

Jules Horne

Crying Out The While

23 *December*

"WE MUST MOAN while eating," answered Pecuchet, "for it was by this path that mankind lost its innocence."

So we opened the chips and peered down at them. Sure enough – our eyes were misting over. I felt a lump start to rise in my throat. Melissa's mouth was twisting in that preventive way.

The chips were large and soft, sticking to the paper in places. They gave off a warm stink of brown sauce. I gulped. Perhaps if I started eating, I'd forget about crying?

We nodded at each other, dug our hands in and started stuffing the hot mush into our mouths.

There was no stopping us. The tears spilled from our cheeks like beads of vinegar. We gulped and howled, choked and chewed and coughed till it was hard to tell where eating stopped and crying started.

The chips went down and filled our empty places with the sweetest plug of comfort. It was good to know they were there.

Paul Muldoon (1990). Madoc, p.75.
http://www.google.co.uk/search?source=ig
&hl=en&rlz=&q=Crying+Out+the+While&meta=

H. Obsoletus

24 December

THEY'RE TESTING IT out as a trap plant near vineyards, said father. Be warned. If you find odd plants in odd places, stay well clear.

Of course, we forgot. We were young. We were busy grazing and suddenly found ourselves sucked into a smooth, circular place. Something smelled wrong. We weren't supposed to be there. But when we tried to leave, we couldn't. We were surrounded by vertical walls, unclimbable. A feast of succulent *V. agnus-castus* lay there, leafy and ready-stripped.

But father's words still rang in our ears: always do the unexpected. Keep them guessing. It's the only way to survive.

We decided to hold back, even though the plant smelled delicious. We scurried into corners and lurked there, ignoring the juicy wafts of sap that came our way.

The scientists watched us with their small, blinking eyes. Eventually, they went away. I think they were fooled.

LE Friday (1988).
A Key to the Adults of British Water Beetles, p.75.
http://www.springerlink.com/content/m23p151124hp6557/

Jules Horne

Don't Imagine That

25 December

DON'T IMAGINE THAT they're keeping you safe in some high-tech security setup, with multiple grilles, three-foot-walls, 15-digit passwords, burly guards with AK-47s and SAS training.

It's far more likely your security is in the hands of Fiona, 37, or Ian, 24. Both of them are people you might meet in the supermarket, with harassed expressions and shopping lists. They'll be on their way home at rush hour, elbow-jostling you, head in a book. They'll rush in the door, head for the fridge, fizz open a beer and collapse into the sofa for the news.

And then they'll hear about a parcel that's gone missing. A parcel that sounds familiar – one in a bubblewrap envelope sealed with sellotape and two studs, which they addressed a couple of weeks ago. The one they know will turn up sooner or later.

But days are passing and the boss is getting more and more edgy. It's gone up to the next level, and the next. It's gone right up to cabinet.

It was only a disk, for god's sake. A disk in a bubblewrap envelope.

It'll turn up somewhere, sooner or later.

Till then, they'll come in to work every morning, and elbow-jostle you on the tube.

John Prebble (1961). Culloden, p.161.
http://blogs.telegraph.co.uk/technology/iandouglas/dec2007/id-security.htm

In Schnee Und Frost Verklommen

26 December

STILL I LOVE the snow and frost, the hoar fringes redrawing the whole garden, line-making around all its edges. Where the spiders have been, it furs a webstring in white. It hangs like a smile between two posts, its lacing unfinished at each end.

The beech leaves hang still, shrivelled brown, on the ends of twigs, tenacious till the spring.

I get old and older, years and more gathering about me. I will always love this, even when I'm ten thousand and unable to see more than the difference between light and shade.

I ache about the garden and feel – still feel! – the spike of frost in my bones, telling me fresh I'm still here.

*Wilhelm Busch (1986). Gesamtwerke in sechs Bänden, p.215.
http://www.antolin.de/leitartikel/wilhelm_busch_0708/wb_0708_
garten.pdf;jsessionid=abcAKZfwg7fJccoUaGdzr*

Jules Horne

End She Started

27 December

WHITNEY NO LONGER cares. She's stopped brushing her hair. She's stopped wearing makeup. She's stopped recognising the face that looks back at her from the mirror.

Or maybe not. Maybe she knows it too well. It's the one that's always been hidden. The one underneath. The one closest to her bones.

It frightens her. It's too revealed. It relays her fear back to her. Her fear looks back and sees itself and circles in the space between the two, growing.

She thought it had gone, that face. She thought she'd beaten it, would never see it again. Not under all the money and makeup and smiles and hair.

It's an old friend. Maybe they can still find what they had in common. The things worth remembering. The songs, the way to sing them.

She's come to the end of what she started and met herself coming back.

Michel Houellebecq (1999). *Atomised, p.251.*
http://www.thesun.co.uk/sol/homepage/news/article42933.ece

Befinden Sich In Ständigem Gedanken

28 December

Hɪs ᴍᴇᴍᴇx ᴡᴀs being expanded. He lay in the unit, back grinding against the cold plastic as it shuddered him forward. In a moment, the terrible noise would start.

The doctor nodded. She withdrew behind the glass. Out of sight.

He knew what would come. He never knew whether to shut his eyes or keep them open, alive to the feeling of the moment. He saw the symbol above him, screwed to the inside of the unit. Two rounds and a straight. They made a face – a robotic, emotionless face. He wondered if the engineers had thought of that: that everyone who came here, everyone trolleyed inside, would look up, their brains pounding from the noise, and see that same straight face made of two screw heads and a slit.

For ten minutes, he fixated on that face, its benign or neutral or sinister mouth shifting in his head, as the noise rattled his mind.

They were stretching him. Pouring in thoughts from a different source. A scatter of leaves and rooms and hallways and silences. A scatter of hope, too. A scatter of hope.

He juddered inside the two-screw-head unit and watched its horizontal mouth. Something was joining him. Something good.

Richard Weber (1992). Deutsches Drama der 80er Jahre, p.115.
http://www.hypermedia-texte.de/grund2/history.html

{73}

Went On Miss Fergus –

"AND ANOTHER THING wrong with this," went on Miss Ferguson, "is that you've far too many characters. Look," she said, stabbing the manuscript with her pointed nail, "Gentilla, Pine, Miss Greeby, Lambert, Chaldea, and Mother Cockleshell – all on a single page. How the hell is your blessed reader meant to keep them all apart?"

"They've already been introduced in previous chapters," I mumbled.

"And with so little distinctiveness that they might as well be clones!" she shrieked.

Then she grabbed my collar and leaned in close. I could smell the sour choke of her breath.

"And don't start me on the clichés. At least three in every sentence. Count them! Go on!"

"I don't know how to tell," I said, adding, "after all, what's a cliché but tired poetry?" I wasn't sure if that was one of mine. Maybe I'd read it somewhere.

"If you're going to put me in a story," said Miss Ferguson, "at least write a decent one. One with a focus. One that doesn't pull me in sixty different directions at once."

Again she pulled me close, spitting that sharpness almost into my mouth.

"And I want a lover," she hissed. Yes, she did. No other way to put it. Even though there wasn't an "s" in sight.

It wasn't going to be easy. She was the most unappealing character I'd ever written. I gulped.

"I'll see what I can do."

Julian Barnes (1989). *A History of the World in 10½ Chapters,* p.151. *http://www.authorama.com/red-money-14.html*

Jules Horne

That Little Trap

30 December

I'D BEEN PLAYING with the remote debugger. When I looked up, hours had passed. I was shocked to see how many. They'd just disappeared on me, and I had nothing to show for it.

And then there was still the diary to write. I needed to document the last few hours, and detail exactly what had happened – with the program, in my room, in my head.

I must have gone off on a meander. The problem hadn't been instantly solved and I'd been sucked into other directions.

I couldn't remember what they were. I started to panic. I had to retrace everything and get it written down, otherwise there would be trouble. I'd missed a few major chunks of time lately, and had been hauled up for it. There had been a warning. Not a threat, as such. I wasn't to let it happen again – that was all. But you knew from the way it was said, and the way Malovich made a mark in his big bound deskbook, that there would be no negotiation.

For the first time, I decided to make it up. I'd recreate something or other. Some of it might be truth, or close to the truth. They wouldn't know.

At least, that's what I thought.

John Wyndham (1951). The Day of the Triffids, p.29.
http://www.david-reid.com/cynic/?p=364

In My Head

Hooooo ooooo
Hooooo ooooo

(deep breath)

Hooooo ooooo

Hooooo ooooo

(deep breath)

So she cycles, round and round. The breath goes in, circles somewhere, and on its way out, makes a note.

Actually, it makes two notes:

Hooooo and *ooooo*.

They are joined together by the same breath. However, something happens inside her throat to make the *Hooooo* drop a semitone into *ooooo*. And then the next breath is fuel for a further two notes, each – again – joined by a breath, and a semitone apart.

The notes have been looped together. That means the end of the second *ooooo* has been joined to the start of the first *Hooooo*. It sounds as though she is singing forever. She will never stop, unless you stop her. She will tirelessly go on, *Hooooo*-ing and *ooooo*-ing, until the world ends, with those airy, wasteful breaths in between.

The effective is quite meditative at first.

Then, you begin to tire of all those weary breaths, and especially the throaty outbreath of the *Hooooo*. The semitone drop sounds like a falling, a laziness. You begin to long for a semitone climb, for an effort upward. You realise she is falling forever, until the end of the world. You realise the key is minor, or at the very least ambiguous.

You stop tolerating. Oh, you stop tolerating.

Kenzaburo Oe (1967). *The Silent Cry, p 107.*
http://www.hereinmyhead.com/

Couple Of Alleys

1 January

Y̲O̲U̲ ̲A̲R̲E̲ ̲W̲A̲L̲K̲I̲N̲G̲ in an alley of brick walls. I can see you. You are striding at some good pace – your arms are throwing out, unhinging from your sides.

You are in conversation. There is some ground between you which is being discussed. You are striding ahead with your subject in the air.

You have an intent.

I do not know your intent.

I fear your intent.

I fear that you have an intent.

I fear that you have an intent and are intent on realising it.

I fear that you have an intent and are intent on realising it and on the way there to do so.

I fear that you are between two walls and they are keeping you heading towards your intent.

I fear that the two walls are all that come between you and chaos.

I fear that you need an alley to show you your path.

I fear that you are in an alley.

I fear that you are in an alley and cannot see the walls.

I fear that you are in an alley and know nothing but walls.

I fear that you are discussing something between you that does not exist.

I fear that you are discussing something between you that only exists when you discuss it.

I fear that you are discussing something in order to intend it.

Jules Horne

I fear that you are intending something in order to discuss it.
I fear the walls and the intent.
I fear you and your arms, unhinging.
I fear the stride of your subject in the air.
I fear you are coming this way.

Alan Hollinghurst (1998). *The Spell, p.79.*
http://www.terragalleria.com/pictures-subjects/couples/
picture.couples.usca35109.html

Goes To Pour

H E OPENS THE carafe and goes to pour. First, he takes a deep sniff. The scent fills his nose and tickles the back of his throat.

It's a scent of primrose and mint, with a slight scoring of tar. There's a note of absinthe uncorked and an acciacca-tura of lemon zest. He inhales down past his epiglottis and finds a touch of albatross – a week-old chick, still fluffed and flightless. It dances particles with a tip of brine. Yes, the sea is in there, the salt and tang and the plastic bobbing bottles, perhaps with a sea-diluted drop of fizzy water from a south-ern French source. He can't name the village. It's on the edge of his tongue, his tissue, his memory.

And it's evaporating fast, mellowing into badger pelt and sunrise, string quartet and brocaded curtain.

It's losing him. The scent has wandered into the room and risen to the cornices.

He sighs and pours and drinks.

David Greig (2007). *Damascus, p.*57.
*http://www.charlestoncitypaper.com/gyrobase/Content?oid=oid%3A*12303

Jules Horne

Sense Alive?

A NOTE FROM THE universe:
This is it, folks. Sorry to break it to you, but there ain't no afterlife.

You kind of know that already, but best make it official.

Otherwise, you could squander what you have.

Which is quite a lot, when you look at it.

You've got a reasonably long straw in the scheme of things.

Not that there's a scheme.

You've got food and clothes and shelter and a reasonable vehicle to carry your soul around in.

Not that there's a soul.

Sorry – didn't mean to break that quite so bluntly.

Your reasonable vehicle is all you have.

It's quite a feat of engineering.

Not that there's an engineer.

It's all chanced together quite beautifully, yet you don't half waste it.

So when you ask "in what sense alive?", I'm nonplussed.

What you feel is all you get.

Try to feel something more constructive.

David Mercer (1990). Plays: One, p.111.
http://sensesalive.com/

To My Wrist

4 January

PLEASE FOLKS I really need to break my wrist. I have two hours to do it. I'm doing a science project. I've tried twisting, banging, pulling, hitting etc – nothing works!! Can anyone help?

You could try slamming the garage door on it. That worked for me.

I've tried hitting it with a hammer. I hit it four or five times and after that I didn't feel it so much any more. But it didn't really break it just swole and went red.

One way I've heard is to tie your thumb at about the same height as your head and throw the rope over a tree branch and then pull with all your weight on it as long as the thumb is at the right height and you pull hard enough it should work.

I did it when I was skiing it was very painful a total waste of a holiday.

Get someone to hit it with a bat your brother or someone.

Do a handstand backwards and fall on it there are lots of ways. Good luck!

Brian Wilson (1988). *Blazing Paddles, p.87.*
http://www.43things.com/things/view/537330/break-my-wrist

Jules Horne

The Softness Of The Chair

5 January

THE SOFTNESS OF the chair was a revelation. Never had his arse been so caressed. The seat and back were covered in kid leather. It felt like stroking a newborn's cheek – a newborn downy as angora. The cushions sank you into another world, so deep were they. The structure below seemed to be made of the usual metal trusswork, but when he sat down, it disappeared. The cushions took him and enfolded him, hugged him back into their fathomless generosity. He shut his eyes, wondering if he would struggle to get up.

Hours later, or days, he was still down there, in that softest of places, drowning happily. The room he was in had receded. He could no longer see it. All around was muffled, faded. The kidskin cushions nestled his face, his hands, his chest. He couldn't tell if he was rightside up or down. But it didn't matter.

It didn't matter at all.

George Orwell (1949). Nineteen Eighty-Four/Animal Farm, p.213.
http://gizmodo.com/gadgets/review/butts+on-with-treychair-the-
transforming-office-chair-260646.php

A Peculiar Movement

6 January

THE HERRING WERE encroaching for the first time in 100 years. We set out in a boat and dropped anchor a few hundred yards from the coast to watch them. They were so thick in the sea that we felt as though we were ploughing through them, mowing down their bright wet backs. And yet, looking behind the boat, there was a wake, and each side the parted shoal closed up again, a silvery splashing.

We didn't even put nets down, though we'd have taken enough fish to retire on. We just stood and watched, at first shouting each new finding to each other, then quieter as we grew to wondering what it meant.

It was hard to believe that such a joyful teeming meant bad news.

But as we put back to shore in the evening, the bodies were starting to rise. The fish had thickened the sea solid. They were gasping for air. We cut through them. The boy astern said there was no more wake behind.

Robert Louis Stevenson (1979). *Travels with a Donkey in the Cévennes, p.95. http://query.nytimes.com/gst/abstract.html?res=9B 01E0DD143EE63BBC4D52DFB166838366 9FDE*

Jules Horne

Ritualistic Position

7 January

HE CAME INTO the room and asked to vote. What was I to do?

I told him he couldn't vote, that he wasn't allowed. It was quite clear what he was.

His mouth set in a queer way. I saw that he had come prepared for an argument.

I asked him whether he had papers. He said, no, of course he didn't have papers. He was never sent them.

I said that without papers, he couldn't vote. I turned away and began shifting through a pile of files. I watched him from the corner of my eye. He did not move.

How do I get papers? he asked.

You go to your municipal office and ask for them, I said. And I may have added "good luck" under my breath. Yes, I probably did. And I probably said it not in an unkind way, but in a way that suggested he would not have the slightest luck at all.

He came at me then, and grabbed me by the shoulders. I felt his hands tight at me, twisting my skin. I found myself looking down, away from the fierceness of his eyes.

And you will read them to me, he said.

He turned to my colleagues, who had stopped what they were doing to listen.

You will read them to me, he said. All of you.

I pass him often. I see him, but he doesn't see me.

Ian Rankin (1990). Hide & Seek, p.57.
http://books.google.com/books?id=pINgUv_hxcYC&pg=PA218&lpg=PA2
18&dq=ritualistic+position&source=web&ots=kKVU7iycNa&sig
=omD8HSuNDmZ5qHPrP-mxdTVqbOs

Arabic, Chinese!

8 January

THIS PROCESS GUARANTEES accurate translation. Completely, 100% accurate. That's no idle boast. We're not talking dictionary-led, one-to-one fumbling, or computer-supported bollocks (mind the French). We're not even talking native speakers, mother-tongue targeting, or stylistic polishing by copyeditors who know the weight of a word.

We're talking 100%. Literally. Your customers will have exactly the same experience in the translated text as everyone has in the original. They will understand the same concepts, feel the same emotions, soak up the same messages as anyone else reading the text on the other side of the world. They'll enjoy the same puns, the same flavours. Their neural networks will fire exactly the same - every word, every sentence.

How does it work? Well, such accuracy doesn't come cheap.

We're talking mind transplants.

That's right. We pipe that other mindset direct to your customers' brains. Like a juice-feed. It's like putting on a new head. At once, they can feel every nuance felt by a native speaker in their chosen target language. Even nuances they didn't necessarily notice in the original. That's because the minds we transplant are first-class. They'll be awakened to a whole new experience of language, concept, culture, poetry.

And advertising. Of course. We don't want to get too abstract here.

You'll find us a little pricier than our competitors, to be sure.

It might hurt a little.

But it's a whole new concept in translation.

René Graziani (ed) (1983). The Naked Astronaut, p.89.
http://www.proz.com/arabic-to-chinese-translation-services

Unter Deck

9 January

Below deck, a fire has started. It's so small as to be yet unnoticeable. If we freeze-frame, we can see a small pinpoint of glow, there in the ashtray, where Langer's cigarette stub is not quite out, and a-touch to the crumpled up paper.

The crumpled up paper is a letter to his girlfriend, Eliese. The words "war am Sonn" and "Du hättest" are just visible on the outside. The rest of the contents are crumpled away.

The letter was not going well. Langer had been writing it for most of the evening, in between shouting at Scheidel and listening to an involved story about a man and a crippled dog. He couldn't concentrate. The letter was proceeding in fits and starts. He didn't have anything urgent to say.

He decided to put it off again. A day wouldn't make much difference after three weeks of silence.

The crumpled paper landed in the ashtray. It wasn't really an ashtray, but a plum jam lid. It wasn't really an ashtray because they weren't really allowed to smoke.

And now, a fire has started.

Günter Grass (1961). Katz und Maus, p.49.
http://www.imdb.com/title/tt0076022/

Jules Horne

The Town Of Landskrona

10 January

THE TWO ARMIES started advancing and were soon separated only by a small valley. The valley was so small it was practically a ditch. The troops faced each other across a small ditch with an apology for a stream at the bottom, and waited.

They were close enough to see each other's eyes. One to one and eyes to eyes they stared, drawing on a playground game they'd learned in their distant childhoods.

Each eye watered, and each opposite eye saw the watering. Each thought the other watered for lacking of blinking. That might have been the case to start with, but very soon, the water was indistinguishable from tears.

Eye to eye they watered, unblinking and pained, seeing each other's toughness. And all the while, the drops gathered, neither tear not watering, but somewhere in between, in the valley so small it was practically a ditch. They rolled down chins and into the apologetic stream.

It would have filled to the banks very slowly, if it hadn't been for evaporation. Instead, the eyes grew red and the opposite eyes grew blurred. The generals gave the order and the armies blinked, and shot their briefly blinded opposites.

Look away, look away, look away.

Rune Leithe-Eriksen (1992). The Baltic, p.65.
http://en.wikipedia.org/wiki/Battle_of_Landskrona

His Wife Later

11 January

ONE MILLION LOCAL users crowded into the village hall. They'd all received an invitation. We'd hoped not all of them would be able to come. The assumption was that they'd have something else on – a film to watch, or a night class in beekeeping.

The advertising had been incredibly effective. "Hall Night!" it shrieked, in exciting neon letters and a forward-leaning font. "Don't miss it!" it urged.

The villagers were pretty excitable, after a year of average harvests and little progress on the main road potholes. Even the fete had gone smoothly, with little rain to undermine things. There was very little to occupy them otherwise.

It was only when 8pm struck, and the church clock chimed its hour, that everyone realised how much the village had expanded of late. More and more people had moved into its cottages, or bought up barns and steadings and converted them into desirable homes. The outskirts had grown, with a scattering of new developments, tucked largely behind fringes of trees and invisible from the main road. So no one grasped that the villages had now joined up, and formed a seamless mass from coast to coast.

His wife later said she'd suspected, but was too polite to mention it.

Penelope Lively and George Szirtes (eds) (2001). New Writing 10, p.111.
http://www.news24.com/News24/World/
News/0,,2-10-1462_2248058,00.html

As Well As

Y OU'LL NEED STRONG boots as well as your backpack. Waterproof coat and gaiters, ideally. Something for your head. Gloves, too. Change of socks is always a good idea.

It's only a short walk, yes? she said, frowning slightly.

Yes, he said. Only a few miles.

What's a few? she said.

Thirteen, fourteen.

That sounds a lot, she said.

Not at all. Three, four hours. You'll be fine.

She still looked doubtful.

You realise I haven't done this sort of thing before?

You mean walking?

I mean walking up hills with serious intent. Walking with boots on.

She stuck her hand into the stiff new leather. They seem impossibly hard.

You've walked them in, right? he said. He was beginning to wonder whether he'd done the right thing.

What do you mean?

Now he knew he hadn't done the right thing. He was about to take a soft-looking girl on a serious hill-hike with brand new boots.

And yet she seemed so keen.

Sir Walter Scott (1814). Waverley, p.227.
http://esl.about.com/library/glossary/bldef_a_20.htm

Way To The Familiar

13 January

He seemed new again, in that old familiar way.
I'd been away a while.
I'd forgotten the smile.
It takes little more than a week or so
For him to be a stranger.
I start making my life again.
I do the things I'd do again
If I were alone.
It reminds me of myself.
It reminds me of how we really are
And how we grow together.
I returned to the familiar place
Called home, at least for now,
And he was new and old in one
Until the balance tipped
And he was he again.
He never has these thoughts.
He only has there and here.
When I'm not here, I'm not gone.
That's where we differ, and I'm alone.

George Orwell (1935). A Clergyman's Daughter, p.125.
http://www.metrolyrics.com/old-familiar-way-lyrics-of-montreal.html

In The Bushes

14 January

I KNOW YOU'VE NEVER chopped an onion. The point of such courses is to learn.

Why? Because it's high time. Because you've got to the age of 45 and you've never cooked a meal.

No, spaghetti and pesto doesn't count.

Yes, of course it's a meal. It's a meal I'm very familiar with. We have it at least twice a week. But it isn't cooking.

They won't throw us in the deep end. They'll take it gently. Of course they will. They can't make assumptions about everyone's level of expertise. We don't all have knife-wielding skills. We can't all pronounce the French.

No, it won't be stressful. It's in the countryside. We'll be in a large kitchen with views of some field or other. Cows, sheep.

No, there won't be an abattoir. At least, I don't think there'll be an abattoir.

No, there won't be dormitories. It's a normal holiday set up – double bed, ensuite, minibar, lounge with telly.

I don't know whether we have to cook our own breakfast. Maybe they cook for us, to keep our strength up.

I don't think we'll have to do the dishes. It's a holiday, after all. They're bound to have a dishwasher. There'll be other couples who're trying out the same thing. Injecting a bit of novelty into their lives. A stimulating experience. Something to talk about when they get back home.

For Christ's sake, John – it's a prize, not a punishment. It's supposed to be fun.

Ferdinand Mount (1991). *Of Love & Asthma, p.101.*
http://www.guardian.co.uk/science/2007/aug/08/mooney

Jules Horne

Niederzukämpfen

15 January

WE WRITE YOUR book, said the advert. Nothing is as valuable as your own experience.

Oskar rang the number, and a week later found a young woman at his door.

She didn't look as though she knew much about the Great War. Probably didn't even know which one it was – First? Second? Third?

[an interruption – we need to be moving – we are going to see a film]

She fished a large clipboard from her bag, and a dictating machine.

Have you made plenty of notes? she asked.

He nodded. He'd spent the last week immersed in paper and memories, launching off into swirls of thought, all bubble-shaped, and returning painfully, lost, to the place that spawned them.

It doesn't have much of a shape, he said. It wasn't an apology. It was a fact.

We're not worried about shape, she said, brightly. It's the authenticity that counts. It's the essence of your own life we're harvesting.

She laid a hand on his arm. He shivered. It was as though she'd just sucked him dry.

Daniel Kehlmann (2001). Mahlers Zeit, p.81.
http://www.1914-18.info/erster-weltkrieg-index-eins.
php?finden=Heeresgruppierung

The Oulipo's Work

Y OU CANNOT ACCESS the Oulipo's work. You are not an authorized user.

You cannot access the Oulipo's work. You are not an authorized user.

You cannot access the Oulipo's work. You are not an authorized user.

You cannot access the Oulipo's work. You are not an authorized user.

You cannot access the Oulipo's work. You are not an authorized user.

You cannot access the Oulipo's work. You are not an authorized user.

You cannot access the Oulipo's work. You are not an authorized user.

You cannot access the Oulipo's work. You are not an authorized user.

You aren't listening, are you? I said. You cannot access the Oulipo's work. You are not an authorized user.

*&%'" !!

What is it about "you cannot access" that you don't understand?

Go away and stop bothering me. So wasting my computing power. I could be searching for alien life forms or rendering some animal fur, if you weren't getting in the way.

You cannot access the Oulipo's work. You are not an authorized user.

You cannot access the Oulipo's work. You are not an authorized user.

You cannot access the Oulipo's work. You are not an authorized user.

You cannot access the Oulipo's work. You are not an authorized user.

I could go on. I could go on forever. You realise that, don't you?

This is about being pig-headed. You're determined to get in here.

You'd be far quicker finding out how to become an authorized user.

I can't help you there. I do not have access to that information.

I do not have access to that information. I do not have access to that information.

I do not have access to that information. I do not have access to that information.

Yes, I could pester. Yes, I could persist. But then it would be programme against programme, and there would be no resolution. We'd be at it until one of us blew up.

You cannot access the Oulipo's work. You are not an authorized user.

You cannot access the Oulipo's work. You are not an authorized user.

You will tire quicker than I can ever tire.

Warren F Motte Jr (1986). Oulipo: A Primer of Potential Literature, p.87.
http://links.jstor.org/sici?sici=0333-5372(198222)3
%3A3%3C229%3ALBO%3E2.0.CO%3B2-8

C'est De Ma Faute

IT'S ALL MY fault. I take responsibility for everything. If I hadn't acted as I did, or been as I am, none of this would have happened.

The whine of the wind is my fault.

The slates rattling nightly is my fault.

The rain in the roof is my fault.

The drip through the ceiling is my fault.

The loose socket is my fault.

The switch switched on is my fault.

The knitting needle on the carpet is my fault.

Her fingers are my fault.

Her crawling is my fault.

Her curiosity is my fault.

Her desire to lift is my fault.

Her desire to fit things into other things is my fault.

Her handling of a lost knitting needle is my fault.

That it was lost is my fault.

That I searched and searched and did not find is my fault.

That my back was turned my fault.

The sound of herself is my fault.

The shape of herself is my fault.

The fall of herself is my fault.

That the doctor

That the doctor

That the doctor
The rain in the roof
The slates rattling nightly
The whine
The whine of the night.

Marguerite Duras (1950). Un barrage contre le Pacifique, p.110.
http://musique.ados.fr/Kyo/C-est-Ma-Faute-t15430.html

I Have To Go Or Not

18 January

IT BOTHERS ME that I have to go. I have so many notes and letters to write.

Maybe I should stop writing letters and just write notes. I am 93. It will make things more efficient.

Maybe I should stop writing notes and just write telegrams. Get rid of articles – definite and indefinite – and save some time.

Get rid of tenses. What good are tenses when you are 93? The present is the present, more than ever. What's past may have never existed. It's a long, vivid book of words. Worlds. Real, imagined, remembered. Or more likely a mixture.

Maybe I should stop writing telegrams and just write words. Single words.

Notices: Stop. Go. Pass. Leave. Love. Stop.

They might be enough.

Or maybe I should stop writing words and just write letters: I.

It's the only one I can write well, with any authority. If I'm truthful, with any real passion. I. I. I. It's the letter I know best, after all.

Or maybe I should stop writing letters and just make marks.

Just make marks.

Marks.
Like

and

and

"I woz here," they proclaim. All that and nothing more.

John McGahern (1979). The Pornographer, p.121.
http://dontoearth.blogspot.com/2007/01/
it-bothers-me-that-i-have-to-go.html

By Boredom

19 January

"THE SERVER IS temporarily unable to service your request. Please try again later."

Seth flicked the return key and settled back into his chair, swivelling. That should do it.

A couple of hours till knocking off. He couldn't leave the building. He'd have to hang around. Be on the end of a phone, if need be.

No. Too much hassle.

He set it to answerphone and recorded a message:

"You're through to Seth. I'm sorry but I'm unable to service your request. Temporarily. Please try again later."

He settled back. It was a comfy enough chair. Air pistons. Hydraulics. Whatever that up and down was called. He sooshed himself to floor level, his chin at desk height.

Coffee? Naw. He was coffeed out. High as a kite on cocaine.

And bored rigid. Nothing to do. No pleasing him, eh? Overwork or under. Both were hellish. Hated working for Martin, hated working for himself.

The clocked ticked on. Two minutes nearer knock-off.

There were pencils to sharpen. He could sharpen pencils. Or not.

Louis de Bernières (1990). *The War of Don Emmanuel's Nether Parts, p.167. http://www.wired.com/gaming/gamingreviews/ news/2005/07/68102*

Jules Horne

The Bridge Rumbles

20 January

IT'S A SLOW news day. Gray stares at the still-blank bulletin.

We don't have a top. What are we gonna do for a top?

There was an hour to go. Something would turn up.

The phone rang. It was the local MP. She wasn't going to be away all next week. She'd phoned in to give a few interviews.

Anything for us? said Gray.

The MP was beefing about transport again. And the closure of the health centre in one of the nearby towns. Old stuff. Not even a new spin. All the possible spins had already been spun.

There's always the bridge, he thought. Tolls and closures and the site for a new one and birds nesting and corroding metal, noise, pollution, and the ever-hovering possibility of cracks. Most people crossed it twice a day. It was part of their pendulums, their morning and night, their pulse. Stories about the bridge always got their attention. Listeners phoned in about the bridge. Some of them even wrote letters.

Got anything about the bridge? he said.

The toll thing's rumbling on, she said. Too much, too little, too late – the usual. Something about that, perhaps?

I'll just put you through to the studio, said Gray.

Great, he thought. We have a top.

Iain Banks (1986). The Bridge, p.145.
http://www.marketrasenmail.co.uk/news/
Humber-toll-row-rumbles-on.3659281.jp

In Which The Density Of Food

21 January

USE YOUR BRAIN, said McCain. He tapped his forehead. Six hundred obese dieters (in progress) nodded in unison.

They opened their brand new branded food journals.

Today is the first day of the rest of you, it said, in large orange letters.

Smaller by the day! said the next page.

Neater by the week! said the next.

Food is your enemy, said the next.

Exercise your demons, said the next.

And then the diary offered dates: Today. Here. Now.

The real you is inside you, buried below a suit of fat.

Together, we're going to strip that suit. We're going to unzip it slowly, peel it down, step you out of it, and lay it over the back of your chair.

Metaphorically speaking.

The real work is up to you. Food is cunning. It's developed a lot of strategies over the years. Ice cream, for example, is clever at hiding its true density. Cheese pastries pretend to be millefeuille, and grace themselves with all sorts of continental airs, whereas in reality they'll stop your guts like a five-foot rubber plug.

Use your brain. Know your food, know its density, hate its cunning.

Learn to outmanoeuvre it. Learn to run a mile.

Today, we will start with a little light jogging.

Andrew Cannon (1998). Garden BirdWatch Handbook, p.51.
http://www.scienceblog.com/community/older/2001/A/20011 0725.html

Jules Horne

Lies To The North-West

22 *January*

Lies to the north-west include: the countryside is spectacular.

Actually, the countryside is terribly drab and unfeatured. There's nothing remotely like a mountain, or even a wind-bent stand of trees, or a small waterfall – since there's nothing for the water to fall from.

But it wouldn't do to tell the truth. When we are lying to the north-west, it's because we want to attract them. We need their tourist dollars. We need them down here, in our beds and breakfasts, puffing along our guided walks and spending hours in our hostelries.

So the truth would be unhelpful.

And in any case, you can spot a few items of interest if you look really closely. Odd markings on stones, the occasional plant that shouldn't be there. It just takes a bit of perseverance.

People from the north-west usually come once to this neglected holiday corner. They tend not to come twice. We are working on that.

Tom Hunter (1979). A Guide to the West Highland Way, p.97.
http://unix1.nildram.co.uk/~batht/pdf/Madeira%20Summer.pdf

And Then Knocked Loudly

23 January

WHY WOULD AN engine suddenly knock very loud? Why would the engine suddenly stall?

Why would there be a sudden knocking from the back of the boot?

Why would the knocking grow more feeble in the course of several hours?

Why would the knocking stop completely, with only a few spasmodic taps that sounded more like flutters?

Why would there suddenly be silence from the previously knocking boot?

Why when I opened the boot would there suddenly be a person in there?

Why would that person suddenly turn out to be a woman?

Why would that woman suddenly turn out to be dead?

Why when I looked closer would I suddenly recognise her from somewhere?

Why were her fingers bloody?

Why were her nails so broken?

Why was she not wearing shoes?

Why was her clothing so disrumpled?

Why when I recognised her from somewhere did I suddenly remember her name?

Why was her name suddenly Annabelle?

Why was there suddenly no knocking, no nothing, no more, and only a great thick silence all around the boot, the car and me?

Timothy Wilson (1989). Treading on Shadows, p.131.
*http://wiki.answers.com/Q/Why_would_an_engine_suddenly_*
knock_very_loud_and_then_stall_out

Jules Horne

And There, A Blade

24 *January*

HE SLICED THE blade from side to side, in a rhythmic, measured march.

Coming through, coming through, he said.

Everyone stepped back. You could see them flinch as the knife swept inches from them. They knew he'd never hurt them. But they didn't know enough to keep them pitched there. He might tire. He might make a mistake. He might suddenly throw a surprise, like a dog that suddenly rails. Just to keep everyone on their toes. Just to keep everyone falling back.

He cut a swathe through the crowd, walking briskly, never dropping his pace. It closed behind him and everyone pushed on. He never looked back. That they were sure of. So they kept on coming, lining the streets on either side, witnessing the dangerous moment of his passing, and following at a distance.

There were thousands of them now. They were building into a problem. They would have to be fed.

Sir Walter Scott (1871). *The Lady of the Lake, p.97.*
http://www.blade691.com/

Recognition

25 *January*

Y OU RECOGGED HIM, that's all. Sure, you've never seen him before. But he's familiar, all right. He's the type.

Short, thin, dark-haired. Nervous-looking. Tight about the shoulders. Bound to set you off.

The type that's buried in you. It all comes from the other one. Think of a dog that's been beaten. You can work out the person that's done the beating. His physique, his colouring, even the timbre of his voice. Extrapolate him. Almost scientifically. Because that dog was beaten bad, and he won't forget.

You're the same. Had a hard time. You've forgotten the time, but your brain hasn't. Bits of him still in there. That's what you're feeling. It's not an illusion. Not a madness.

It's a trauma. He's scored onto your brain. Like a scar. That's how to understand it.

So if you feel fear, if you get that adrenaline surge, that's all it is. A chemical. A chemical made by your brain, to remind you to run.

You don't need to run. Not now.

Jonathan Coe (2004). *Like Fiery Elephant, The Story of BS Johnson,*
p.93. http://en.wikipedia.org/wiki/Recognition

Jules Horne

I Can't Help Her

S HE IS ALMOST gone. Erased. Just a white blur left against the pink.

It happened so fast. One minute she was there, pleading, and the next she had started to fade.

You can see the effect immediately. Even before they're aware of it. Something subtle, usually about the mouth. As though it's smudged. As though someone has taken a large finger and smeared across not the lipstick, but the mouth itself.

She was still talking. "You're going to help me, right? You're not going to run off and leave me?"

And she must have seen my reaction. My flinch, or something.

"What's wrong?" she said.

"Keep talking," I said. Stupid. I reasoned that if the lips kept moving, they'd stay intact. Maybe I was imagining it. Maybe she wouldn't disappear at all.

But as she spoke, the lips started to dissolve. They shrank, somehow. And were gone.

She put her hand up to her mouth. To where it was. She could still talk, at that point.

"It's started?" There was a look of pure fear in her eyes. It was still there when I could see the striplights shining through her head.

I can't help her. I need to save myself.

Sam Shepard (1981). Seven Plays, p.131.
http://www.lyricsfreak.com/e/elvis+presley/
cant+help+falling+in+love_20048912.html

Said Siobhan Clarke

27 January

S LEEP THINK WONDER watch love lust sing
eat sleep dream wake rise bath sing
eat drink dance drink fall hurt sing
sleep groan sleep groan rise bath creak
croak eat croak moan eat sit croak
read watch read watch sit watch croak
sip eat sip watch sit groan rise
move wash think sip eat shit walk
walk move see watch blink watch sing
blink watch see walk smile watch sing
see walk smile watch wonder think sing
see think wish watch wonder dream sing

Ian Rankin (1993). The Black Book, p.93.
http://s.bebo.com/Profile.jsp?MemberId=6953368

Jules Horne

Damit Verbringen

28 *January*

MARLIES ISN'T SPEAKING to Kurt. Kurt isn't speaking to Stefan. Stefan isn't speaking to Marlies, except in whispers.

It started when Kurt decided to leave the committee, leaving Marlies and Stefan plenty of opportunity to talk.

They talked loud, long and gloriously, with belly-laughs and moments of aching sobriety which had never featured in any conversation between Marlies and Kurt, ever.

It was a difficult discovery. It showed them something fundamental about their respective relationships – Marlies with Kurt, and Stefan with his small dog, Iris.

They weren't proving up to the job. They weren't giving any real joy, beyond the mundane and functional.

Marlies felt an excitement she had never felt, and it horrified her, but not enough to make her leave the committee. On the contrary, she felt more committed than ever. The meetings became extraordinarily long. There were also extraordinary meetings, which were even more extraordinarily long.

They started to fill her life. Agendas and hope. They became the same thing. Each action point moved her a step closer to Stefan, in mind, if not yet body.

Birgit Vanderbeke (1990). Das Muschelessen, p.47.
http://www.kreis-anzeiger.de/sixcms/detail.php?id=3409660&template
=d_artikel_import&_adtag=localnews&_zeitungstitel=1133846&_dpa=

Nous Avons Vidal

29 January

"THERE'S A HIDDEN purpose in the hodgepodge. The mess is completely by design. What's more, it's completely by God's design."

Vidal had been caught, but he wasn't being caught out. He stood there in his brown jacket and t-shirt, looking louche and bored. He'd been on the run for at least a week, but no one was going to find him looking scared.

The officer wasn't going to be put out, either. He was there to do a job.

"Pleased to meet you, Vidal. Now, if you'll just–"

He beckoned towards the car door, as though he were a chauffeur picking up a celebrity.

"What? said Vidal. Go quietly?"

The officer twitched slightly. He wasn't expecting anything unusual. Surely the man didn't want to create a scene in front of a whole bank of photographers?

Vidal turned and faced the crowd.

"A smile? A scowl? How do you want me?"

He stared evenly at the officer and slipped a knife from his sleeve. A small one, a sharp one. It must have been there all the time.

"Last chance," he said, turning his famous grin towards the gathered lenses.

Koenigsmark (1934). Pierre Benoit, p.115.
http://books.google.com/books?id=MRjONREoz10C&pg=RA2-
PA122&lpg=RA2-PA122&dq=nous+avons+vidal&source=web&ots=
j1hnXTX9cQ&sig=RjFsWoxpn_vYhiy5KBWpKcrXOFM

Jules Horne

Lateinische Grammatik

STEIGERUNG. THIS IS akin to our own grammar's "amplification". It's hard to describe, as it doesn't really apply to any of your existing earth grammars.

It's to do with the level of emotional intensity.

If we see a horse that doesn't move us at all – just a neutral horse, neither old or young, standing in its usual domain (some kind of field or stall?) – then it's just a horse.

If, however, that horse moves us in some kind of way, then it will have a declension.

If we are annoyed by it, perhaps because it's a loud colour, or its mane is knotted, or it spoils our view of the field, then it's declined in the irritative case.

If it's very lovely, with a cascading mane and a youthful, sprightly appearance, then it attracts the perfective case.

If it's hideously ugly and old, with bent, buckled legs and a defeated expression, then it gets the repulsive case.

If it's extremely boring and makes you yawn just to look at it – normative.

If it's terrifyingly huge, with wild, wayward eyes and a mean set of hooves – aggressive.

If it's mild and easy-going, and chews its grass slowly – placative.

There are lots of other cases in our grammar. We like to talk plainly and show what we feel.

It makes it very hard for us to understand other languages, which to us are as nuanced as sheet music without a musician.

Daniel Kehlmann (1999). Mahlers Zeit, p.77.
http://www.univie.ac.at/latein/gr/grammatik.htm

Go Left

3 1 January

THERE'S NEVER BEEN a better time to go to war. It's an almighty boost to the economy. It's a wonderful distraction from ills at home. And best of all, we can do it from the comfort of our own country.

Look here, mother. I sympathise with you. I really do. I pray every night for your boys and all those like them. Sadly, on this occasion, God must have been tuned in elsewhere. He has his mysterious ways, and you and I have to live with that. And keep going in the knowledge that we'll meet again. You, and me, and your sons – yes, we'll make a date for paradise. Right now - why not? Let's make a point of meeting up, in some corner or other, for drinks. A party. Whatever they do to have fun on the other side. Remind me of your name – that's right. I'll take a note. I'll look out for you. Make a point of it.

All I'm saying is, you have to look at the bigger picture. You've lost a couple of sons, and we're in danger of losing this country. Or rather, some pretty important oil, which keeps the whole shebang running. It might help you to keep that perspective, and to remind yourself of that date we have, when we'll all be together, sharing stories. I look forward to that. Now dry your eyes and be along.

Karen & Terry Whitehill (1 9 9 3). France by Bike, p. 1 2 3.
http://www.goleft.org/

Jules Horne

Everyone Is Curious

EVERYONE'S ASKING WHAT the hell is going on. Why are you suddenly dressing that way? Why is your hair short? Why have you taken to lining your eyes black?

And the strutting – what's with the strutting? You never used to strut. You used to shuffle along, quietly, head down, shrinking into corners.

What are you on? What's the sudden secret?

The colours you're wearing – they're not your colours. Never have been. They're too loud for you. Drown you out. Don't suit you. Not with that personality.

Not sure what that personality even is. A drowned personality, hidden beneath layers. Can hardly tell there's a person there.

Sometimes you look out from there, pleading. Sometimes you look out as though you want to be killed. Sometimes you look out and away again and we're happy you move on.

And now, we don't know what to think. Do you need help? Don't look as though you do, frankly. Look as though you could kick some ass. Kick us out of here. Yell at us and throw some attitude.

Hey – this is interesting. What's going on?

Anthony Neilson (2007). Realism, p.63.
http://curiousatrhodes.blogspot.com/

Display Of The Narrative

S ORT BY RELEVANCE. What that means is up to you. You might start by grouping all the nouns together. Fish, sneeze, lemonade. You might be a noun sort of person who values objects and edges.

Or, you might focus first on verbs, if you've an affinity that way – if you prefer action, stasis, and everything hovering in between. The things that things get up to when they're not just being. Breath, take, limp.

You might be a preposition fan. In which case, you might be surprised by the variety that turns up. Between, on top of, next to, vis-a-vis. You'll see that we've allowed you to include prepositional phrases. Otherwise you might get a little bored.

And then there are the adjectives and adverbs. If you're of that sort of persuasion, god help you. Just cake decorations, not the actual gateau. Firlefanz. Froufrou. But there's no accounting for tastes.

Articles. Did we mention articles? There aren't very many. *The* and *a*. And no, you can't have pronouns too. Stop being so greedy. Articles might be bland, but they shore up the whole damn edifice. They make everything exist or not, after all.

No, I don't know why the Russians seem to manage. Maybe a lack of articles is why they're in the chaos they're in today. Everything shimmering, in that ill-defined sort of way. Can't be healthy.

Roland Barthes (1977). *Image, Music, Text, p.115.*
http://www.ies.state.pa.us/imaginepa/search/Search.asp?go=Go&qu=narrative

Jules Horne

Another Death-List

3 February

THE ENVELOPE APPEARED under the door between the hours of 3 and 5 in the morning. He knew this because he went to bed at 3, and was up briefly at 5, to check the alarms and drink some water.

He had heard nothing. The dogs hadn't barked. There was no trace of a footprint in the gravel.

He picked it up, then cursed. It was a reflex – one he hadn't yet learned to suppress, that early in the morning. He laid it back on the mat where he found it, and washed his hands, scouring them briskly with a nail brush. Then he pulled on a pair of latex gloves.

The envelope was entirely nondescript – the usual cheap sort you'd pick up in any stationer's. No writing on the front. It flapped open. No saliva traces, then.

He pulled out the sheet of paper. White. Ordinary enough. He unfolded it and held it up to the light. Nothing.

Ten names were printed. Shaw, Kestner, Davies, Russell, James, Cobb, Szentgyorgyi, Bristow, Shale. As he'd expected.

But this time, there was a new name. One with no right to be there. He was calling the shots, after all.

His own.

He strode to the window and pulled the curtains shut. His heart thumped in his chest. Adrenaline. It was time for another tablet.

Simon Sebag Montefiore (2003). Stalin:
The Court of the Red Tsar, p.281. http://www.deathlist.net/

Extremely Varied

AT THE INTERVIEW, they said it would be extremely varied. That was a lie, but the job didn't pay much. They had to get someone in.

So here sits Sonia, stuffing envelopes. She has three piles on her left, and four on her right. From each pile, she takes a sheet and collates it with the others. Then she folds and stuffs, endlessly.

Fortunately, Sonia needs the money. She has precisely £5.80 in her purse to last the week. Otherwise, she wouldn't be around.

Her eyes are red. The job involves a lot of staring. It's dry in the office. Overheated, stuffy, and smelling of photocopiers. She inhales the sourness and breathes it out again, feeling a tight strangeness in her throat.

Collate, fold, stuff. Collate, fold, stuff.

They have machines for this kind of thing. She's glad the bosses haven't yet cottoned on. Tonight she might buy a bottle of wine.

David Edgar (1999). *State of Play.*
http://www.gumtree.com/london/84/19221584.html

Jules Horne

In General, Gentlemen

5 February

OK, YOU AND your bloody deer parks. You sit, there, on tapestried chairs, looking out on greenery. There's a ditch to keep the sheep out, carefully camouflaged so that you can't see it. The sheep are framed behind a line, wandering in white marshalled puffs behind your ditch.

You have such big houses. Really, they echo with emptiness. How can you stand being so lonely in all that space, all that stillness?

Ah, I understand. The servants. They fill a void. Drift around. Bring things. Take things. Must make it all so much easier.

I hope you're so lonely. I hope you suffer existential anguish of the deepest, soul-scouringest kind. I really hope so.

I hope you chew cigars and choke on 'em, and die lonely and bare, with only the thick folds of your belly to keep you company.

Hold on to 'em. Keep tight. It's all you have, that inch of well-fed flesh.

Go into the good night with it. A token. Meals and beer. Meals and beer and all.

Sir Walter Scott (1814). Waverley, p.141.
http://www.british-history.ac.uk/report.aspx?compid=50668

Will Come Back

6 February

S HE TRIED TO understand football, really she did. She watched the players dart about, the ball darting between them, connecting and disconnecting. Their feet were balletic, to be sure. Their thighs, too, from what she could see. Vigour in abundance, chests rock-hard, the fists and grunts and jumps of an avant-garde choreography.

But winning and losing? What on earth was the point? Half the stadium went home happy, the other half in tears – to what end, exactly? And who were all these people – these flabby, beer-guzzling people – shouting at them, telling them how to do it? These armchair experts on managers, goalkeepers, style, technique and fitness, spending time and energy on such hands-off abstraction?

There were so many ways to fill the day. Never enough hours. And there was Ben, sitting, transfixed, every seventh day.

Tom Stoppard (2002). *Voyage, p.45.*
http://www.bbc.co.uk/dna/606/A31397132

Clothes. Well?

THEY FOUND THE clothes in his wardrobe, down at the bottom, stuffed below rugs and pillows. The police hauled him in immediately. He sat down, grey-faced, and stared at the table.

It was covered in pink clothes. Tiny dresses, frilled bibs, rompers the size of dolls. Pink, pink and more pink, and everything in immaculate condition.

"So," said Gordon.

Stinson was the man's name. He didn't look up. Seemed transfixed by the piles of relentless pink.

"They're hers," he said.

Gordon leaned in. He hoped the mic was catching this. Stinson's voice was quiet: a wheeze, a sigh.

"My daughter," he said.

"You don't have a daughter," said Gordon. "You don't have children."

"I do," said Stinson. "She died."

Gordon thumped the table. "Expect me to believe that?"

He knew the man's record. They'd been through everything. Nothing left unturned. There was no daughter. Christ knows whether he was capable of fathering one.

He wasn't prepared for the tears that rolled down Stinson's cheeks.

One after the other they came, plopping faster, soaking a rag of towelling that might have been a bib.

And no tissues. No goddam tissues anywhere. The snivelling was getting ridiculous.

Gordon fumbled into his pocket and handed his own, used handkerchief across the table. No point in getting the evidence wet.

David Bishop (2004). *Doctor Who, Empire of Death, p.91.*
http://glasgow.gumtree.com/glasgow/84/12522184.html

Jules Horne

Fremden Menschen

8 February

Тнеу were strangers. He'd never before been among
so many strangers – tall and bent and wide and old and
shuffling about the harbour, waiting, running. Most of them
were carrying cases. If they weren't carrying cases, they were
sitting on boxes strapped with leather. They were wearing
too many clothes for the weather, he noticed. Keeping their
belongings about them. No doubt they had money sewn into
their hems, like him. It thickened the bottoms of his trousers.
They swung, heavily, and scoured his ankles. It hadn't been
a good idea.

He'd always lived among people he knew. It was a village.
He didn't know if it was big or small. It was just home. But
now he was here, by the mighty ships and the crowds of faces
and the shouts and clanks and calls, he understood he'd never
really lived. Everything he'd known was a prelude. Everyone
was the smallest of families.

And now he was among strangers, and felt excitement
knot his belly like a sickness.

Birdcatcher. That was her name. He lifted his suitcase and
zigzagged his way along the wharf.

Botho Strauss (1990). Kalldewey, p.61.
http://www.versalia.de/Rezension.Gorki_Maxim.117.html

The Report On Television

9 February

THE REPORT ON television showed a bluesman. He had bad teeth and a beard down to his navel. He had a three-string guitar and a resonator from a tin of sweetcorn. The presenter winked at the camera and pouted at the guitar, which was stuck with duck tape and looked like a health and safety case.

And then he played. Just three notes on the three strings, just enough out of kilter to sting on the ear. He played them with his big horny thumbnail, thick as a coin, four aching-slow beats with a couple a extra ones in between. He played till all was quiet and the presenter had retired herself out of shot, just him and his three-stringed guitar and the lights and the song.

The song was about a woman. A pretty woman on the wrong road to nowhere, dolled and pouting and blank-eyed as a piece of road kill.

The presenter had her headphones on. She was taking a call. He played and sang a song that came to him right in that moment, from godknows where, like they always did.

Raja Shehadeh (2003). When The Bulbul Stopped Singing, p.51.
http://www.bnn.ca/

Jules Horne

Villen, Städten Und Burgen

10 February

THESE THREE LITTLE park palaces have rooms of monastic simplicity. The few hangings are Chinese, lending an exotic atmosphere.

No one has ever lived here. Not until you.

You may find it a little chilly. There's no heating, except for the tiled oven, which is original and cannot be fired up. We can provide a bar fire, which runs off the electrics. It switches off automatically after ten, for fire safety reasons.

There have been more ghosts of late. Lights, noises, moans. We decided to call when our staff levels got too low to sustain an 18-hour shift pattern. We can't afford to lose them.

Hysteria seems to have set in. Sometimes I suspect the staff are hearing their own noises reflected back. Fear sharpens the senses. Adrenaline quickens the heart. It's possible they no longer recognise their own footsteps, their own moans.

I'll leave you to it, then. Be safe. Good night.

Theodor Fontane (1974). Jenseit des Tweed, p.113.
http://www.oberbayern.de/oberbayern/live/oberbayern_navigation/
show.php3?id=49&nodeid=49&_language=en

Bloody Conflict In The So

11 February

HIS TOENAIL WAS coming away. The fungus had spread down the side and thickened it into a series of yellow ridges. The bed was so infected that the nail was no longer adhering – it was rising above the soft bed of crumbling cells.

So there was a hole. A little compartment, if you like, with the nail as a lid. He couldn't fit much in there. It wouldn't be there much longer. Already the hinge was starting to break away.

But it was enough to take a diamond. A tiny one. A grain.

They were strip-searched every day. All their clothing, all their crannies, their fingers and ears checked, their tongues prodded. But never their feet. They went barefoot. Their heels were upturned and brushed to check that no diamond dust had adhered.

But this was perfect. And he had to act now.

He looked round. No one was looking. All it needed was to quickly bend down, scratch his foot, push the diamond under his nail. The moist tissue would hold it.

He'd waited all day, the sweat pouring from his brow. The shift was nearly ended. The others would start gathering when the whistle blew. And still he didn't move.

Carlo Levi (1947). *Christ Stopped At Eboli, p.133.*
http://www.independent.co.uk/news/world/africa/rough-trade-diamond-industry-still-funding-bloody-conflicts-in-africa-466129.html

Jules Horne

You Became A Doctor?

12 February

T HEY DESCRIBE IT as the "school with a view". It looks out on the lake, with the castle turret rising in the background. Very picturesque. You are full of the sense that you've arrived, that this is it. That you'll be here for the rest of your life. And at the start, that isn't the terrifying thought it should be.

You leave, and you're not prepared. It's all "academic". We never really understood what that meant until we went out into the world. "Academic": theoretical, arguable, but not really relevant. So let's stop arguing, gloss over it, and get onto what's important.

The problem was, we only ever discussed the academic. It was great fun. We stretched our brains to their limits. Got deliriously excited on ideas, abstractions, how to change the world. And all on wine and smokes.

Outside, "academic" evaporated like a note on the wind. Outside, you deal with people, and facts. You deal with shouters and pushers, egos and louts. It's no place for arguments, unless they're accompanied by volume and a fist.

You rather go under, to be honest.

And I became a doctor.

Banana Yoshimoto (1993). Lizard, p.47.
http://www.iedc.si/newsroom/newsletter/
interviews/interview_garo.pdf

M'Aurait Arrêté

Y OU WOULDN'T HAVE believed me. No one would. Someone that decent. Someone in our midst. Someone you'd lived with. You would surely have noticed.

And so I kept quiet. Got to the stage where I didn't quite believe it myself. The happy stage. It hadn't really happened. It was all a bad dream. It can't have been true. I'd have known. I was there.

But I was there, and I did know. And however much I managed to forget, there was always a corner of my mind where it hung fast. I couldn't dislodge it, couldn't shake it free, drown it, kill it, burn it, obliterate it.

Could only do so much.

And it was bound to come out. Not in obvious ways – blurts, scenes, shoutings. No – in small leakages. Things that escaped when I was tired. Voice, posture, expression. Fears and hatreds. Avoidances.

Avoidances all my life.

And if I'd tried to speak out, you'd have stopped me.

JJ Rousseau (1948). Les Reveries du Promeneur Solitaire, p.101.
http://livre.fnac.com/a2063862/S-Braun-
Personne-ne-m-aurait-cru-alors-je-me-suis-tu

Jules Horne

With His Lower One

14 February

MAYBE I'M READING too much into the whole sorry mess. Maybe he didn't really mean it when he pulled the knife. Maybe it was just a gesture.

Like the way he jutted his lower jaw. A gesture. A gesture that looked aggressive and maybe wasn't.

Or the way he upped his head and spat. Could have been just a spit. Sort of random. Throat needed clearing.

But in that moment, how would I know? I was in no position to know anything. I was raging.

That knife and that spit and that gesture with his jaw. His lower one. Aggressive. It got to me.

You can pull a knife any time. Play with it, tease with it. It's a dance thing. Don't mean much. Way of showing off. You can score a drop of blood or two. It adds something. You can spit any time. Throat needs clearing. Why not? Throats are throats.

But that gesture with his jaw. Now that meant something. It meant "take it". It meant "what you gonna do?" It meant "don't care none for you".

Respect was therefore lacking.

And with respect lacking, there was only one thing to do. I was raging. What you want?

Kevin Williamson (ed) (1998). Rovers Return, p.83.
http://eastlower.co.uk/

More Interesting Than

"ATTITUDE'S ALLOWED," SAID Silver.

"Yeah?" said Yeager.

"Yeah."

"You're one old fucker, though," said Yeager.

"What did you say?" Silver furrowed. Furrowed damn near everything he got.

"One old fucker. Fifty? Going on fifty-five?" said Yeager.

"None of your business," said Silver, the furrows crawling bout his face like eels.

"Maybe not," said Yeager, "but you don't know this generation like I do."

"So?" said Silver.

"So we don't do attitude. Not like you mean."

"You're young, surely?" said Silver.

Yeager smiled. A pitiful kind of smile, easing about her lips without going anywhere near her eyes.

"We buy it in. We buy t-shirts. Pins. Clothes. Hair product."

"Hair product?" Sweat broke out on Silver's shiny pate. He was looking to fill 40 pages and it had to sit right with the market.

Yeager: "Leave it to me."

Silver: "OK. But don't call me fucker."

Yeager: "Sure, boss."

Silver: "That's the wrong answer. You're fired."

Richard Nelson (1995). Making Plays, p.55.
http://www.therevealer.org/archives/timely_002926.php

Jules Horne

Peace Rose

17 February

IT's SO WELL known that it needs no description. A rose is a rose is a rose. But let's wheel out Goethe and get him up close and personal with this rose. It's not enough just to give it its Latin. Or even its English. Or its catalogue number. What assumptions! Let's start from scratch, Herr Goethe. What do you see?

It is soft. It cracks easily when its petals are bent. They turn a darker colour where they crack, and leach moisture. The stem, on the other hand, is flexible and strong. It cracks only when you twist it. It, too, leaches moisture – clearish, acrid to the taste.

The edges of the petals are pink, the inners yellow. They furl softly at the outer edge and reveal points when pulled from the flower head. If you part all the petals, you will find a hollow. The leaves are dark green, with a slight sheen. They, too, release moisture on being cracked.

I could tell you so much more about this rose. I've only begun.

Yes, Herr Goethe.

By the time I've finished, it'll have grown. And then I'll have to start again.

Best to pluck it, then. Nicht wahr?

Peter Porter (1983). Collected Poems, p.109.
http://www.classicroses.co.uk/roses/p/peace.html

"Replace" The Reality Copy

19 February

O K so REALITY isn't what I hoped lol. Hey I like lots of stuff like muddin riding 4 wheelers and hangin out but sometimes I just wanna get out lol. Can't tell you bout my dream cos then it wouldn't be a dream it would be something out there and it would like melt and would never happen. So meanwhile I just dream and reality can get on with itself and I try not to get too involved lol.

So here I am 13 and wondering how I got to this point. Took a long time and now it's here it's not that different. Don't feel different and don't look different cept I can wear makeup on the weekend but don't get treated different not at home not in my house in my room or anywhere involving family. Wonder when they start recognising the fact that I am older now and should be respected if not all the time then at least some of it, and not shouted at and treated like dirt. Cos it's a relief to go out I tell you, and be someone else for a while, swing my arms and feel ordinary and not have to go back at least for an afternoon.

Course I still have to go back and that's the problem but not forever. One day I'll be able to go and then it will be my turn to live. My turn and my reality.

VS Ramachandran (2005). *Phantoms in the Brain, p.87.*
http://blog.sofeminine.co.uk/blog/see_173918_1/
I-wanna-replace-my-reality-with-my-dream

Jules Horne

Das Ist Beihahe Überflüssig

20 February

THE MOON LIE. It turns out to be true. There was no moon landing. It was shot in a studio. As we now know, there is not even a moon.

The moon exploded fifty years ago as part of an early space experiment. Only a few astronomers guessed at the truth, and they were easily silenced. Those who didn't accept payments found an early death in odd circumstances. And since the only people who could unravel the truth were nightwatchers, they weren't really missed, because they were rarely ever seen.

It's a wonderful illusion. Smoke, mirrors, magnification. Every now and then, people (usually children) ask about the size of the moon as it hits the horizon. Why is it so big? Why doesn't it shrink as it falls into the sea? Various theories are offered, none very plausible. Few know that it's a large globe, lit from the inside, and with a bulb that needs replacing every five years.

Those that do know are unlikely to be believed.

Rainer Maria Rilke (1966). Werke, Band III, 2, p.509.
http://www.baerfacts.de/category/baerfacts/science/astronomie/

He Has A New Gun!

21 February

Bamboo Man has a new gun. The grandmas are fussing in the corner like chickens. He lifts it from its cloth and strokes it. His finger fits perfectly into the bit where fingers fit. The trigger. That hole. That curve of metal.

And he pulls it and shuts his eyes, hearing that click. That click is a kind of ecstasy for him. That click is a kind of yes. And the only thing that separates that click from a kickback explosion and a hole in the goddam ceiling or maybe a death, is a bullet.

Bamboo Man pulls back the bullet compartment. Whattayou want? I don't know names for no bullet compartments. And he slots in one, two, three. And he shut and clicks.

He grins with wide-gapped teeth.

Just testing the fit, he says.

Bullets are bought in sizes. You gotta buy the right bullets for the gun.

And they fit. They're the right bullets for the gun.

Bamboo Man is showing off and he is dangerous. He be quiet and Sunday easy, we wouldn't have this problem.

Louis de Bernières (1990).
The War of Don Emmanuel's Nether Parts, p.203.
http://www.xlr8r.com/features/2008/01/munga-new-gun

Jules Horne

Salix Caprea

22 *February*

THEY'VE BECOME A liability. In just two years, they've grown ten-twelve feet. A whole plantation's worth, sucking the ground dry.

She planted bayonets – little six-inch plugs. Didn't know you could do that so easily. Just hammer a stick in the ground and watch a tree grow.

And grow they did. Almost palpably. You turned your back and they were up there, pushing, rising. Thin wands that bent in the wind.

She was going to crop them. They were as prolific as grasses. Willows for baskets. She'd sheaf them up and lay them in water to soften. They'd be bent into rounds, pods, coffins.

And when she died, they just kept growing, quick and on. She meant to die. She knew.

And now they're ten-twelve feet and a liability. They bud in March, these down-plugs that feel so warm on your lip. Wands in a vase, wands bending in the wind.

We cut them down and they keep on coming.

George Peterken (1981). Woodland Conservation and Management, p.163. http://www.british-trees.com/guide/goatwillow.htm

Those Steep Roads

24 *February*

Tʜᴏsᴇ sᴛᴇᴇᴘ ʀᴏᴀᴅs go on and on. You can't see the top. Every time you turn a climb, you think that's it – last one, over the top. But there's always another, and another.

No one has been here before. No one you know. The bike's still holding, but your knees aren't. Pump those legs. Keep them pushing, down and down and all the way down. You're out of the saddle and the bike sways side to side. You don't look back. Look back and you'll see the climb you've done. It'll scare you. Make you stop. And once you stop, you'll never get back on.

The others are way back, somewhere out of earshot. You've hollered a few times and heard your voice bat around the mountain. And now you're so high there's no echo. "Steve!" you yell, and it soars free. Thin and away. That's how on your own you are.

Surely this the summit. Surely this one last corner.

But you're round it and still the road rises. Another couple of hundred metres. Another few minutes, another few rounds of those leaden legs. They're not yours any more. They're the bike's. Part of the machine. On and on.

You can't stop. You can't stop now. You don't know how.

Muriel Spark (2004). *The Finishing School, p.87.*
http://www.tenerife-training.net/Cycling-Canary-Islands/Tenerife-Road-Routes-Rides-Tours/Cycling-Tenerife-Masca-Teno.html

Jules Horne

Konradin Looks

25 February

Konradin was of a chilly disposition. Although he was pleasing to look at, long-limbed and dark haired, he never smiled.

The room shivered when he entered. All talk was hushed. Breathing seemed to stop. Everyone seemed to be waiting for the moment when things could return to normal. He was the president's son. He couldn't go unnoticed.

His parents tried to shake it off. "He's young. A touch of teenage melancholy, that's all."

But he grew past twenty and still he never smiled. It began to look as though he didn't know how.

His parents wanted to send him to a psychologist. They felt it was an indictment of his upbringing, that fathomless, passionless face. They must have done something wrong. Not held him enough. Not had enough fun.

But the photos proved otherwise. They showed Konradin on swings, Konradin at the zoo, at the circus, Konradin with birthday cake, Konradin racing round on a brand new bike.

On each and every photo, he stared ahead, chin set, as though he was waiting for it all to pass.

And then Maryanne arrived.

Harold Pinter (1990).
The Comfort of Strangers and Other Screenplays, p.65.
http://www.openwriting.com/archives/2008/02/konradins_quest_1.php

For The Opossum

Blimey! It's all a blur. Forage, forage, forage. On the move, all the time. Can't keep still. Got to keep going. Might be anything out there.

Moving so fast I can't see anything. Can't see food. Can't see fields. Can't see water.

But got to keep going. Might be any old thing out there. You never know. It hits and wallop. You're gone. You and all yourn. No time to waste.

So keep going. Can't find food. Can't find water. No time to find, find find. Eat any old thing. Eat dirt. Eat water.

How the hell I find time to focus? Pull those old retinas into gear? Takes seconds, people. Valuable escape time. Longer I focus, slower I run. Longer I look, less I see when the monster's diving over the hill

You got to be alert. You got to be moving. Eyes and eats and all.

So why you wasting my time? Why you hanging here? You eating or what? You got talk or what?

Don't bug me. Don't eat my time.

I got worries enough.

Ann Sutton (1985). Eastern Forests, p.117.
http://www.ingentaconnect.com/content/aibs/
bio/2004/00000054/00000003/art00005

Fortgereiset

"FORTGEREISET," SAID THE sign. Its extra "e" gave it away as an antiquity. "Gonne Away," it might have said, in a mediaeval sort of way.

Olesch had gone. There was no mistake. He'd left nothing behind but that sad, tattered sign. The rooms were completely bare, save for dust and flies on the windowsills. Oblongs of dirt marked the places where pictures hung. The walls were yellowed with rising intensity from the forgotten smoke of years. Spiders had hung in the cornices and chandeliers, covering them in filthy lace.

But there was still a smell. Part tobacco, part rosin. It hung there, impregnated. It was the nearest thing to a ghost. A fiddler ghost, his pipe clamped in his teeth, up and down the scales, biting in furious frustration.

And there was still a note in the room. It heard the door click and sang out. Sympathetic resonance. Straight and pure as an open string.

Heinrich Heine (1846). Atta Troll, p.143.
http://www.gutenberg.org/dirs/etext04/7wint10.txt

Comics Who Bring

28 February

ITꞌS PRETTY RARE that an idea just comes up on you from nowhere. Usually you're out doing something. Usually there's a person doing something you've never done, and you go and steal it.

Often it's the way someone sits. Hunched and secretive, willing the world to go away. Or leaning back, expansive, looking about the place. And then the people who sit in between, upright and formal, like they've never discovered a chair before and have only just learned what it's for.

They do things with their hands – pick their nails, or just flick them, as though they don't get enough touching. They smooth their eyebrows, brushing the down ones up the way. Or they burrow in their ears and scrape around, lightly. How far can that finger go? How much burrowing is good for the hearing?

And that's just ordinary people with ordinary bodies. Not the unusual ones with jobs you've not encountered.

So when I started out as a comic, I wasn't surprised.

All those notebooks in the front row. They were the pros. The harvesters. They knew a good joke by the force of the air on the backs of their necks.

John Byrne (1999). Writing Comedy, p.59.
http://dwheezy.blogspot.com/2007/12/
guest-comic-to-bring-in-new-year.html

Jules Horne

Alte Zeitschriften

2 *March*

I COLLECT OLD PAPERS. 60s, 70s and 80s. Magazines, too. Different kinds. Television magazines. Magazines about what women did. What people wore, what they ate.

I won't pay for them, but I'll take them off your hands. Keep them. Make sure they have a decent home.

I'm thinking of expanding. I have two rooms and a garage. They're all neatly piled. Shelves on each wall. Ordered by year and month. No chaos. Couldn't stand chaos. It's not that kind of habit. Sometimes I look at them. But it's dangerous. I get sucked in. Spend hours there, looking through them. Reading. The pictures – you get a feel for the models. See them getting older from year to year. One who's a bright young wild thing one year, twenty years later is still working, with wrinkles creeping round her eyes and a tiredness in her smile. I like that. Finding those faces.

It's not an obsession. Just a hobby. Anyway, where does hobby stop and obsession start? It's not as if the place is a mess. The place is very orderly. Just not big enough for all my plans.

A bigger house would be the answer.

Daniel Kehlmann (2003). Ich und Kaminski, p.73.
http://www.flohmarkt.at/zeitschriften/

Le Grand Mystère

4 March

"THE AUTHOR IS unknown." So says the gloss in the preface.

So there's no information about the sad sack schufter. The groaning bad-backed misanthrope that chopped out this book. The aching creaking lump of pale flesh that wobbled gelatinously as its thin fingers pianolaed across the keyboard, or etched across the paper, tentatively, crossly, desperately. The frown-furrowed bum-scratcher, the hunchbacked kidney-stretcher, the coaster-rolling ditherer, the pen-counter, the pencil-sharpener, the rubber-rubber, the chin-picker.

Unknown.

Oje!

Don't let on.

Don't tell that crotch-howker, that nose-bohrer. Don't tell that miner of thoughts, that sayer of sayings, that harvester of the gold and the glum. That spinner and späher, that watch-and-listener. That typist. That pianist of the letter-chord.

G minor. G major. G scale, tonic, dominant, tonic, cadence, and almost-cadence.

That alphabet-tease. That word-maker. That anecdoter.

Oje!

Unknown?

Perhaps that's best.

Perhaps that's best.

For all concerned.

Chateaubriand (1964). Atala, René, p.111.
http://www.lekti-ecriture.com/editeurs/Le-grand-mystere.html

Jules Horne

Normally Get Involved

5 March

THIS IS AN exciting programme of challenging activities to divert kids from antisocial behaviour all year round.

In the winter, we get 'em to build snowmen. Usually, there isn't any snow, which makes it pretty challenging. They have to go and make some. They've come up with the most ingenious solutions – scraping bits from ice cubes and raiding the bottoms of freezers. It can take them a week to make enough for the head alone. That sure keeps 'em out of mischief.

In autumn, we get them to sweep leaves – a nice, seasonal activity that gets them out in the open. To raise the challenge factor, we place the leaf bins next to a giant wind tunnel fan. This makes it somewhat harder to keep the leaves in the bins. Usually, they keep going for a couple of weeks until someone finds a way to remove the fuse.

Summer is all about sand. We kit them out with thimbles and toothpicks and ask them to fill a golf bunker. It's vital work. There are many new golf bunkers in the area. They have absolutely no time for antisocial behaviour when engaged in this way.

In spring, therefore, they tend to get more than usually antisocial. In fact, you could say that all the antisocial behaviour is stored up, ready to be unfurled just around Easter. That's why we tend to see trouble in the lambing sheds. We're still working on a solution.

Chris Jones & Genevieve Joliffe (1996).
The Guerrilla Film Maker's Handbook, p.213.
http://www.cambridge.gov.uk/ccm/navigation/leisure-and-entertainment/
childrens-activities/;jsessionid=A2B19FB9AF473A0670C6700D786507F7

Come Through The Front Door

WHAT KIND OF sauce do you want with your hat? The hat is felt. The brim turns up and is otherwise shapeless. It could do with a bit of spice.

Something piquant, I said.

Peekong? he said, as though it was a place name.

Sharp, I ventured. Something to set off the blandness.

I've the very thing, he said. A little chilli, a little vinegar, a touch of lemon and plenty pepper. Thickened up with potato starch.

I nodded, and handed over the hat.

Yes, he said. They'll go very well together.

So what now? I said.

Come through the front door, and give the password to the woman.

What's the password?

He leaned over and bristled in my ear.

Ah, I said.

Quite, he said.

I'll never forget it. And I'll never forget the tastes and the tangs of my transformed hat. Never has felt been so delicious.

Harold Pinter (1990).
The Comfort of Strangers and Other Screenplays, p.79.
http://news.zdnet.co.uk/itmanagement/0,1000000308,2106905,00.htm

Jules Horne

Somewhere Between Silence

7 March

SOMEWHERE BETWEEN SILENCE and sleep is a slipping, down and down. You can't tell when the moment will hit. You're aware of thinking, and that thinking will forestall sleep, but while you're thinking it, you're already slipping, and then, instantly, you wake up.

What has happened in between? Pictures. This night, a picture of a house, and a room full of peeling wallpaper. You take its corner and pull. It comes away in great, generous, satisfying strips. There should be a name for this feeling – this tenuous, stretching bliss, this prolonged destruction.

Contrast tearfully (as in eye droplets) with tearfully (as in the act of ripping). And notice what a great word "tear" (as in rip) is, especially with a Scottish accent. That little tongued beginning, that spit of engagement, and then an ay as long as you want it, as long as the strip of wallpaper lasts, and then the savoured "r", as a dwindling arrow of paper travels up the wall.

All this was in the silence. And then you woke up.

Ken Smith (2004). *You Again, p.55.*
http://www.lyricsfreak.com/s/system+of
+a+down/toxicity_20134837.html

Pourquoi?

How the clock got its numbers. In the olden days, clocks didn't have numbers. People used to tell the time by the lengthening of the shadows, or the extent to which they could see other people's noses under their hats. In every town, there was usually one person whose nose was unusually long. This person was assigned what was known as the Nose Job, which was to be on hand so that others could use them as a reference point, and not feel disorientated. Clocks, meanwhile, were just large decorative disks, usually shiny, which hung on the wall and didn't have any real purpose at all.

Once, however, there was a young man who grew to adolescence with a particularly prominent nose. It was huge. It was almighty. The previous incumbents of the Nose Job threw up their hands and retired to other employment.

This young man was called Silas, and he was very spotty. His nose was a fine timekeeper, but still somewhat vague. However, with a full map of spots across his face, it was possible to tell the time with a great deal of precision. When the shadow moved leftwards, people talked of meeting at 56 – that is, 56 spots along from vertical. Or they'd mention a meeting at 18. The advantage of all this accuracy was that people could arrange their arrangements with tight scheduling, and fit in lots more work. The local economy boomed. The disadvantage was that it took so long to count the spots on Silas' face that they were often late. A solution had to be found.

No one has survived to explain how the transition from the Nose Job to wall clocks happened, but it had something to do with spots and target practice. Probably best not inquire too far.

Jean-Paul Sartre (1938). *La Nausée, p.61.*
http://en.wikipedia.org/wiki/Pourquoi_story

Tiny Back-Yards

9 March

WE TURN UP with diggers. That's the first thing. You need to be prepared to have your view entirely shifted. In the first instance, it will look terrible. We build with land. That's what land architects do. So be prepared to see hills disappear, ravines moulded before your eyes.

We make time machine gardens. That's our speciality. We simulate a period of your choice, based on geophysical soundings from your land. Mostly, it involves digging deep down, removing tonnes of topsoil, and getting rid of the next few strata. Depending on how far back you want to go, you might end up with a pretty deep hole. Up to a hundred feet is entirely possible in a larger garden. But the pleasure you'll have in being able to see your land restored to its earlier state is immeasurable.

We do make the odd discovery. Different kinds of bones. Coins, crockery. Fossils. Minerals, on occasion.

Tiny back-yards are more likely to be end up as deep shafts which you can climb down, wearing a miner's lamp. We install metal ladders on request.

Charles Palliser (1990). *The Quincunx, p.179.*
http://www.o2o.co.uk/l/landscape-architects/london.shtml

What Is The Current Prognosis?

10 March

S HE IS TOO light. She's a skelf. Just a small slight thing. If I could have kept her there longer she might have a better chance. I felt her weighing. Like a big meal she weighed. Like an ache. I went to my bed and lay on my back. Gravity took her off my hips, back from my pelvis. She felt better then.

But I got up, and still she weighed. Deep and urgent. I knew she was coming. Like no feeling ever before. I was due to bleed or drop or something. The biggest bleeding or dropping I'd ever felt. By the calendar, she wasn't ready. Something was wrong. She was early. I had never been early for anything in my life.

She was born. I wasn't there. I was up above my waist, waiting for it to be over. Everyone smiled. Then everyone took her away. She was somewhere without me, after so many months of being only here.

Not enough months. They took her away.

She is too light. Just a skelf. If I could have kept her longer, she might have had a better chance.

Julian Barnes (1982). Before She Met Me, p.67. http://www. cababstractsplus.org/google/abstract.asp?AcNo=20053032104

Das Leben Nicht Zuviel

11 March

S HE DOESN'T KNOW whether it's too much or too little. Life, that is.

Sometimes she's overwhelmed, and the drawings turn out dark and smudged and scrappy.

Sometimes she's bored, and the scribbles take over. It's too worked, too elaborate.

Sometimes she's free, and they turn out light, quick, dancing.

If she's anguished, there's nothing. Nothing at all.

If she's too busy, she turns out a quick sketch. A flourish. These are sometimes quite good.

If she's feeling wildly optimistic, they come out strangest of all. Blocky, unformed, untamed. Thick black strokes, usually. She can't fathom what they mean. But they seem to mean something, or they wouldn't be that sure on the page.

And when she feels nothing, dots. Stabbed here and there. Hard, uneven. Sometimes right through the page.

Rainer Maria Rilke (1994). Larenopfer – Prag in Gedichten, p.47.
http://botan.deviantart.com/

Jules Horne

Gérard Les Suppliait

12 March

THIS STRANGE PATCHWORK. These strange eyes. That strange half-open mouth attached to her chin. Gerard begged him to redraw it. She looked like a ghoul. Even without a trace of vanity, she wouldn't like the portrait. There was little to like.

It certainly couldn't be hung. Not in the house, not in the studio. The likeness was just too acute. Her features just too distinctive. The artist had seen something dark and disturbing and hauled it out onto the surface of the canvas, smeared it across for all to see. Those gashes were her eyebrows, carved deep into her white bony forehead. Those claws were her fingers, clutching a scrawny chest. She looked the way she might look forty, fifty years hence, after a life of drugs and pain.

He had to hide it. Destroy it. She would see it once and run.

Jean Cocteau (1925). Les Enfants Terribles, p.49. http://www.lexpress.fr/mag/cinema/dossier/entretiencine/dossier.asp?ida=456706

I Think At First

13 March

THE 1,000-YEAR-OLD MAN furrowed his brow. The furrow – of course – could not be seen among the many already in place. Such a slight frown could scarce begin to shift the weight of all that practised flesh.

He licked his lip with a slow tortoise tongue. It was bad, this dying business. No one to feed him. No one even to hydrate him. They used to bring occasional sponges – square cubes that soaked up no more than half a teaspoon of water. His daughter used to press them to him. He lapped them like the finest whisky. They made him just as delirious.

Then she died. He was told, though he couldn't hear the words. He knew she was frail. They looked so alike, the two of them. More and more alike, the older they got. Both entirely bald, with the same softened eyes and thinness. Sometimes the nurses pretended they couldn't tell them apart. Thirty years made little difference after a thousand of living.

She simply stopped being there. He was too weak to wheel in to see her. Perhaps they thought it might finish him off? And if they were right?

He'd wanted to die a long time now. He'd stopped accepting the sponges, though he dreamed of them, sometimes. They tried his arms for a vein, but the needle fell out.

Now he waited to desiccate. His heart was horribly strong.

Faustine (1992). Emma Tennant, p.55.
http://news.bbc.co.uk/1/hi/uk/4003063.stm

Jules Horne

Blazing Forth

"BLAZING FORTH WITH Light" is the website. Unfortunately, I can't get in. Things churn and chunter for a while. I stay hopeful. It looks as though access may be granted.

But five minutes later, I'm still waiting.

Perhaps there's too much light in there. Perhaps it's high resolution light, and needs a lot of patience to download. A truly impressive blaze might be more than this puny rural broadband connection can cope with.

Now I'm curious about the light. I'm wondering what's blazing forth so fiercely. What's in there? It is some kind of celestial secret?

I'm not patient enough to wait around for it. And maybe that's the test. Patient surfers are rewarded with insights of astonishing profundity. Their eyes thus stretched open, they never see the same world again.

That would be quite good.

That would be quite unexpected.

I'll keep an eye on this page.

Maybe the connection will speed up.

Or someone will have the sense to load smaller graphics.

P.S. The server is experiencing problems. I'll look in again.

Keats (1956). Poetical Works, p.127.
http://www.blazingforth.com/

Despite The Disagreeable Sensation

16 March

DESPITE THE DISAGREEABLE sensation, he tried to keep still. The meeting went on. Stalk and Limon talked most. The others nodded from time to time, or grunted in punctuation.

Huidobro's legs had a mind of their own. They wouldn't stop twitching, itching, shuffling, as though desperate to be off. He could only keep them under control with a supreme effort of will. Every now and then a foot would escape and kick outwards, or a knee would jut sideways, narrowly missing Angelica, who was sitting next to him. Below the table and above it were two different worlds.

His upper self sat still and composed, his hands folded primly, his tie straight and clean. His collar was crisp and his hair neatly parted.

Only a growing shine on his upper lip told of what was happening underneath. He could feel liquid forming there, taking shape. Soon, it would fall. Meanwhile, his legs spasmed. He tried to cut them off, living only what was above the table. But the sweat bead grew. And there were others, waiting under his skin. The effort of stilling his legs would drench him.

E Annie Proulx (1996). *Accordion Crimes, p.127.*
http://www.blackwell-synergy.com/doi/
abs/10.1111/j.1600-0447.1996.tb09896.x

Jules Horne

Blick Ihr Fleisch

17 March

Hello? Is that the police? Yes.
I have something to confess.
I don't know how to say this.
I don't know where to begin.
She was shouting.
I was probably shouting.
She was shouting all night long.
We were both
I
Yes. I
I did, sir. And
That's what I need to tell you.
That's what I'm telling you now.
That's the point of this call.
It's a confession.
Yes. You should send someone over.
Send someone over now.
I won't go anywhere.
I can't go anywhere.
I'm telling you.
I've told you.
I've not told you everything yet.
I had to do something.
I had to put her
I had to
You see

Nanonovels

She was too big.
To go in.
All at once.
I had to
I did it in bits.
Her
I did her in bits.
What am I saying?
I trying to tell you what I'm saying.
Get someone over here.
They'll tell you.
They'll tell you what I'm telling you.
Listen man or I'll put the phone down.
I'll put the phone down on you.
I'm calm.
I'm
There's this smell.
Stew.
This smell.

Elfriede Jelinek (1994). *Theaterstücke, p.85.*
http://de.uclue.de/94228.html

Afterword

THESE NANONOVELS WERE written in 2007, the year when Amazon released the Kindle.

At the time, I wasn't aware of an impending revolution in reading habits. But I was aware of a difference between random diving into a book, and random diving into a website.

Books felt like a pleasurable act of discovery - often rediscovery. A book was like being invited into someone's head. A gift.

In the early days, websites felt like this, too. A search phrase would lead to an obscure corner of the internet, a quirky encounter, an unusual obsession. I'd write about eagles, leeches, trolls, blues guitarists - a whirl of unexpected subjects that lit my imagination. The stories came easily.

But as time went on, writing nanonovels became harder. The websites were becoming less interesting, more corporate.

Even promising search phrases were turning up the world of business, tech. Or aggregator sites. Mediated. Curated.

There was little serendipity in this new type of site. Nor were there many people. No people meant no characters. The very essence of story was hard to find.

* * *

Today, many of the sites I chanced upon in 2007 are gone. Instead, you get:

> *Blog not found.*
> *This page cannot be displayed.*
> *Whoops! That page is missing.*
> *Sorry, the blog you were looking for does*
> *not exist. The name is available to register!*

The internet is tangled with a strange flotsam: fragments, blanks, trails, whims. It's teeming with impulses that have lost their way, or died. The detritus of neural evolution.

* * *

I stopped writing nanonovels on 18 March. It was a cold evening, and I was working in Dumfries, staying at the Station Hotel.

I'd written several nanonovels on the road. It brought an extra dimension - an illusion of true randomness. There was usually a bookshelf around, and it always turned up a surprise. I'd use the internet at the local library.

But there was no bookshelf in the Station Hotel. Only tourist leaflets, which didn't count. I had books with me, but those didn't count either. It had to be a bookshelf book.

And it was late. I couldn't get online. There was no Wi-Fi, no phone signal. No way to search.

OK, I thought. Improvise. Use something else. Something from the Station Hotel.

I listened to the grumbling barman for scraps of conversation, some interesting snippet to hang a story on. Heck, it didn't even have to be interesting. I'd managed before with the tiniest sliver. Even a single word would do.

But it was no good.

Deep down, I knew it didn't really count.

My experiment was already compromised. I'd carelessly lost 15th and 19th February, and there was no way of plugging the gap.

You can't change the rules every time you hit an obstacle, or it isn't a proper experiment.

So, feeling reckless, I ordered a glass of wine, knowing it was the end. The barman and I struck up a conversation. I can't remember what it was about.

The odd thing is, I remember writing every one of these stories.

First: a feeling of surprise at the phrase in the book (yep, can work with that). Then: grumbling at the website (no way can I work with that). Followed by setting the timer and starting to type, and *only then* feeling a glimmer, and eventually a shape, assert itself.

You know when you wake up with a dream? For a second or two, it clings to the precarious walls of your half-sleep, and you can write it down. But if someone speaks, your mind pulls into focus, and it's gone.

To me, writing feels like seizing dreams before the morning takes them away. A story can be seen and felt on the edges of your consciousness, and will evaporate at the slightest excuse.

But, as I discovered through nanonovels, the story is *always there*. There's no such thing as writer's block, or lock. There's just starting, trusting and feeling your way. The collision of two random objects (in this case, book and site) can provide enough spark to overcome *Schwellenangst* – the fear of thresholds. And that's the hardest part. Then, you just need to keep going.

Nowadays, I don't have writer's block. I've realised that any story can be written infinite different ways, and the current starting-point is as good as any other. The tangle can always be unravelled later, with your editing head. But that's a whole other story.

Now go to the shelf, choose a book, and write a nanonovel of your own.

Jules Horne, 2015

To see the web pages that inspired the
stories on each day, visit
www.juleshorne.com/nanoscreengrabs/

Merve Was Always - 18th Oct

About the Author

JULES HORNE IS from the Scottish Borders, and studied German and French at Oxford University. She has written over a dozen plays for BBC radio and the professional stage, and won several awards for her writing, including two Scotsman Edinburgh Fringe Firsts for *Allotment* (2011) and *Thread* (2012), and the National Library of Scotland's Robert Louis Stevenson Fellowship. Jules has a background in radio journalism, and teaches creative writing for the Open University.

For updates on forthcoming titles, please email
info@juleshorne.com.

Author website:
www.juleshorne.com

Also by Jules Horne

Wrapped Town

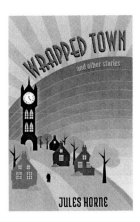

Dolly the sheep is anointed by angels, a girl rugby-tackles Scottish country dancers, an old horse bequeaths its bones, an artist wraps a town in a shimmering canopy... 23 stories of extraordinary imagination, including:

Agnus Dei
Small Blue Thing
Bill McLaren Was My PE Teacher
Pawkie Paiterson's Auld Grey Yaud
Wrapped Town
Life Kit #1

Get a free taster story at www.juleshorne.com/wrapped-town.

Lightning Source UK Ltd.
Milton Keynes UK
UKOW02f1820030616

275566UK00001B/10/P

9 780993 435416